THE BACHELOR AND THE BREAK-IN

ELISE FABER

THE BACHELOR & THE BREAK-IN
BY ELISE FABER

Newsletter sign-up

This is a work of fiction. Names, places, characters, and events are fictitious in every regard. Any similarities to actual events and persons, living or dead, are purely coincidental. Any trademarks, service marks, product names, or named features are assumed to be the property of their respective owners, and are used only for reference. There is no implied endorsement if any of these terms are used. Except for review purposes, the reproduction of this book in whole or part, electronically or mechanically, constitutes a copyright violation.

OAK RIDGE

Bottles & Blades
Beauty & the Boardroom
The Bachelor & the Break-in
Ballrooms and Blackmail

PROLOGUE

BROOKS, FIVE YEARS BEFORE

FUCK, she's beautiful.

A dream as she walks toward me in a wedding dress, the fabric bright white against the rich dark green of the pines surrounding us, caressing her body in a way that mixes innocence and sin.

It clings to breasts I've dreamed about, strokes over hips I've imagined grasping as I thrust deep, splits at mid-thigh, giving me a glimpse of legs I've fantasized about parting wide then wrapping around my hips as I push deep into the tight, slick heat of her.

Mine.

Mine.

All I've ever wanted.

The woman I'd burn the world down for.

The thought ricochets through me so violently that I freeze.

That I know.

Know.

The truth.

The reality.

The...future.

But by the time I process it, what that reality means for my —*our*—future, she's there.

Her bright blue eyes glimmering with love and hope, with tears of happiness.

She...is beautiful and good and...

I'm a monster.

I'm going to destroy her.

And suddenly, instead of mountains, I see my father's study.

Dark wood. Locked doors. Men who come and go in the middle of the night, speaking of awful things that never should see the light of day.

Files that I wasn't meant to see, to know about, to open.

Accounts that shouldn't exist.

Journal entries documenting despicable acts in cold, businesslike language.

I thought I had changed all of that after my father died, thought I'd made amends and pulled our family business out of the shadows. But none of what I nearly killed myself to enact makes the least bit of difference.

Not today.

Not with those photos still so fresh in my mind—her soft smile, the brightness in her eyes.

Not with Pascal's warning in my ears—she'll become leverage. Or worse, a message. A *lesson*.

Yes, I'd burn the world down for her.

But the truth is, I can't protect her from mine.

No matter the silence I promise to keep, the obedience I give, the deals I make, the blood that stains my hands, they won't stop.

I can only become the villain in her story, let her believe I never loved her.

Let her *hate* me.

Because that hate may be the only thing that keeps her alive.

Her hand finds mine and she steps close, fingers tightening in that soft way of hers, silently telling me she's here.

Her plump lips are painted pink. Her freckles are softened by her makeup. Her lashes look longer than normal, darkened with mascara, and they don't need the help. They already rest gently on her cheeks when she sleeps.

"Dearly beloved, we are gathered here today to..."

I nearly jump out of my skin at the soft female voice coming from between us. The officiant is holding a book even though it's clear she has her spiel memorized, even down to the timing of pauses, waiting for chuckles or laughter or whatever feedback she normally receives from a wedding ceremony.

But there aren't rows and rows of chairs, filled with loving family and friends.

There aren't many voices to lend their approval to the quiet jokes and idioms.

Just two stoic witnesses—one my bodyguard, who I trust with my life...and hers, and the other my best friend, Jace. Who I trust just as deeply.

The mountains are behind us.

A narrow swathe of pine trees surrounding us, their branches intertwining to form a canopy overhead.

It's a peaceful place.

Her place.

And I'm going to ruin that too.

Boom!

Thunder rattles through the air, vibrates through my chest, my stomach. It shakes the pine needles overhead, dislodging glittering orbs of moisture that sprinkle over her skin, her hair, sparkling like diamonds even as they raise goose bumps in their wake. Above the trees, clouds gather, drawing together, darkening the sky in what feels like seconds.

A darkness that is suddenly split by a flash of lightning.

Fat, wet drops of rain begin plopping to the ground, turning the dirt to mud as they splatter onto my head, my suit.

Her beautiful dress.

Laughter fills the air—and it's painful and beautiful all at once.

Because the sound that utterly captivates me in this moment is also what drew me to this sweet, gorgeous, *innocent* woman, what coaxed me to ignore every single instinct I had to stay far, far away from her.

Briar's laughter is not a sound I deserve to hear.

And I know it's one I won't hear again.

Not *ever* again.

Not after what I'm about to do.

She laughs again as she tilts her head back, the drops caressing her face, her throat, soaking into the bodice of her dress.

The officiant stops, closes her book, glancing at us then up at the clouds. "Should we stop?"

"No!" Briar says, slipping one hand from mine and opening it, the droplets splashing onto her palm. "I love the rain!" she cries, flinging her arm wide, embracing the drops as they collect on her hair, darkening the blonde strands, straightening curls I know were painstakingly arranged not long ago.

A pause from the officiant. Then, lips twitching, Briar's utter joy impossible to resist, she reopens her book.

Briar's eyes slide to mine, buoyant with joy. "This is perfect," she whispers as thunder booms again.

As lightning cuts across the sky.

As rain continues to fall.

"Isn't it beautiful, Brooks? How the rain washes everything clean for a fresh start?"

"You're the beautiful one, Raindrop."

The memory of those words, her body cuddled close, her hand in mine, her face going soft when I gave her that nickname slides through my mind, sending pain lashing through me.

Pain I deserve.

"Perfect," she whispers again, her damp palm coming to mine, fingers wrapping tight again.

No.

It isn't perfect.

It's my nightmare...and it will soon be hers too.

Because I'm going to ruin everything.

Before I can say something, can find the strength to pull my fingers from hers, the officiant continues,

"Do you, Brooks Saxton, take this woman to be your lawfully wedded wife, to live together in matrimony, to love her, comfort her, honor and keep her in sickness and in health, in sorrow and in joy, to have and to hold, from this day forward, as long as you both shall—"

"I don't."

The words are ripped from my soul.

Spat into the air.

Shock reverberates back.

From the officiant.

From the witnesses.

From Briar.

"I don't," I repeat.

Fingers convulse around mine. "You're supposed to say I do," Briar whispers.

My lungs seize. "No," I say. "I'm not."

"Brooks—"

I slip my hands from hers. It's not easy, not when she's clinging to me so fiercely. Not when she's looking at me like...

I can't allow that thought to form, can't allow the words to coalesce in my mind.

I might do something that's worse than this.

I might...stay.

"I don't," I say for a third time.

Though this time I pair it with putting distance between us, enough and so quickly that I see it break off a little chunk of that innocence, that sweetness, that essence that is purely Briar.

It shatters as it falls to the ground.

Gone.

Forever.

"You're supposed to say *I do!*" she says again, more forcefully.

I shake my head, commit her ravaged face to memory, know I need to hold that image tightly so I don't give in, know it's the only memory of her I deserve to have.

Then I turn away. Turn from the sputtering of the officiant, turn from the shattering beauty of the only person in the world I've ever loved.

I move toward Jace and Pascal. They've been with me from the beginning.

Long enough to not question anything.

"Brooks," Jace begins, moving to block my exit.

Fuck.

Or Pascal has, anyway. Jace has always been a stubborn fuck with a proclivity for doing what he thinks is right.

I ignore it, ignore him, and look to my bodyguard. "Pascal," I say quietly as I flick my eyes in the direction of Briar.

Luckily, he doesn't argue.

Only nods...just as footsteps echo across the earth, louder

than the rain, which is coming down in sheets now, drenching me, the trees, the earth.

Briar.

"Brooks!"

Pascal steps behind me, intercepts Briar before she can touch me.

Because if she touches me, I may lose my resolve.

"Brooks," Jace says quietly again.

I just look at him.

He sighs, clamps his teeth together, his eyes piercing into me, silently telling me he knows this is a mistake.

But he doesn't comment further, and when I step around him this time, he lets me go.

"Brooks!" Briar shouts again.

I start walking.

Keep walking.

Down along the narrow winding trail, following the faint imprint in earthen ground that Briar knows by heart.

Her place.

Our place.

I keep walking—out of her life.

I think for forever...

It turns out, I'm wrong.

About so, *so* many things.

ONE

BRIAR, ONE WEEK LATER

I WAIT for him to come back.

That's my first mistake.

Sitting on the ground among the trees near the trailhead for hours before eventually sheltering in an old hunter's cabin I never paid much attention to.

Because whenever I was here before, I was too busy getting lost in the beauty around me.

Too busy loving Brooks.

But all I see now is darkness.

And now I've spent a week waiting for him to come to his senses, to walk through the door, to tell me this has all been some sort of horrible mistake and he's so damned sorry.

He'll beg me to take him back.

And I'll make him sweat—but only for a few minutes.

Because I love Brooks, love the life we've built, the man he's become—

Except that man looked at me with ice in his eyes just before he walked away from me on our wedding day.

And he *hasn't* come back through the door.

He hasn't come back *period*. Not that day, not over the last week, not today.

After Brooks's car pulled away, Jace tried to get me to go home with him, to dry off and warm up, to change my clothes and take a minute.

But I refused.

I *fought*.

And eventually, he left me in the rain, in the trees. Though, not for long. *He* came back...and carried me bodily into the cabin, stocking the place with some groceries, blankets, and fresh clothes—clothes I refused to change into until this morning.

Because I was holding out hope that Brooks would come back.

The letter beside me on the bed makes it clear he won't.

It contains information about an account in my name, an apartment, also in my name, and strict instructions not to come to *his* house.

He won't see me.

He'll have security remove me if I so much as approach the gate.

Because I don't need to go back—all of my belongings have been packed up and delivered to my new apartment.

He's boxing me up and shipping me off.

Discarding me.

My lungs hitch and my eyes fill with tears.

But this isn't the first time that's happened to me, isn't the first time I've had to start over.

I know how to survive.

I leave the letter on the bed, slip my feet into the sneakers

Jace brought, and though I want to leave *everything* behind—a kernel of hate for anything that involves Brooks growing in my stomach—I know I need to be smart. So, I pack up the clothes, the food, even the envelope of cash—though it makes that kernel inside me grow. I tuck them all carefully into a bag, along with my purse.

Then I leave, hiking my way out of the mountains and down into the little town.

I take a bus to the city.

I find a place to stay. A job.

And for a while, everything is fine. I'm sad. I'm heartbroken. But I'm alive and safe and moving forward.

Eventually, though, even that bit of peace is broken.

It starts with a woman with model-like looks and long blonde hair approaching me, telling me of a "fabulous opportunity," and when I blow her off, a different approach is made by a man who doesn't like it when I tell him no.

At *all*.

That's when the harassment begins. When my life starts falling apart—one friend, one job, one apartment at a time. Until I'm desperate and alone, and when I'm ripped out of my bed in the middle of the night, I know I have no choice but to follow the orders given to me.

To survive, I do things that haunt my dreams, that fill me with regret.

And all the while...

That kernel of hate inside me continues to grow.

TWO

BRIAR, FIVE YEARS LATER

I NEVER THOUGHT I would be this person.

But...when it comes to the choice between doing something right and moral, and surviving the next few months, I know I don't have any options.

Know I stopped having choices years ago.

On a rainy mountaintop I thought would be the beginning of a happy life.

Instead, it became a nightmare.

My nightmare.

I adjust my gloves, know I can't risk leaving behind even a trace of evidence that I was here.

Hating that I *am* here with every fucking fiber of my being.

"Just suck it up and do it," I whisper.

Because once it's done, I never have to set foot in this place again.

Never have to look out over the peaceful rolling hills surrounding the estate and remember, never have to walk through the gardens I spent so much time in, and wish things were different. Never have to see rooms with the big windows and the bright, cheerful wallpaper I picked out, and hurt so deep inside. Never have to walk up the winding staircase to the tucked away reading room where I could while away hours and hours, getting lost in fairytales I thought were my reality, and know—

My life doesn't work out that way.

I'm not a heroine in a fairytale.

I'm just...disposable.

"Enough," I mutter.

I tug at my beanie, making sure it completely covers my silver blonde hair. I used to love it, used to love the unique color, long and sleek and bright like moonlight, used to love the way...

He loved it.

Loved the hunger in his eyes when he would stroke his fingers through the strands, loved how it would catch on his beard when he leaned close and inhaled the scent of my shampoo, loved the way he would wrap a piece around his finger in an absentminded motion when we were in bed together, talking about everything and nothing.

Because I loved all of that so much I had brushed it obsessively, carefully detangled each and every knot. Oiled the ends. Used a protective spray every single day. Slept only on silk pillowcases.

That stopped being my life on that rainy, heartbreaking mountaintop years ago.

Afterward, I let my hair get so bad, so matted and tangled, I had to cut it all off.

And today, it's more nuisance than asset.

It's why I hacked away at the strands with a pair of rusty scissors I found in the dumpster behind a thrift store, cutting enough off so I could shove the rest of my hair under the beanie and the distinctive color wouldn't give me away.

As rough as they looked, the scissors were surprisingly effective.

Then again, sometimes the best stuff never makes it to the shelves, and those discarded treasures, the items no one sees value in, are what I seek out.

Because I'm one too.

Or, at least, that's what Brooks used to say.

My throat tightens, but I ignore it—ignore the fact that I'm one of those discarded items.

Because he didn't see me as a treasure.

I was just trash casually tossed aside.

Slamming the lid on the past, I check again that my hair is tucked up into my knit cap, that my gloves are fully covering my hands and secured in place by the long sleeves of my black sweater. My leggings are dark and go straight down to my ankles, an inch of which are exposed. I scowl, even knowing I can't do anything about that—I'm tiny, but I'm wearing another thrift store find and the children's leggings are doing what they can. Still, I tug them down, try to cover the slight gap of skin showing.

I know the security system.

But...I need every advantage I can get.

So blending into the shadows.

Wearing all black.

And gloves.

And tucking my hair carefully into my hat.

And hoping the distraction Angela promised to create pulls the guards away for long enough for me to slip past them.

And—

"I'm stalling," I whisper softly. And I am.

Because the self-preservation portion of my brain can't

imagine I'm doing this. Then again, the self-preservation portion of my brain has shriveled up into nothing over the last years.

Lockpicks in my pocket.

It's just after two in the morning, so the guards will be tired.

Along with the cloudy night, the new moon, and a diversion to pull them away?

This will be my only chance.

I squint at the screen of my analog watch—another thrift store find—then up at the house. The shadows shift slightly, and, yup, there they go, the guards pushing away from the wall, suddenly on high alert before they take off running.

I move before they disappear around the corner, knowing I have to risk it or I'll be unable to clear the wide expanse of lawn, get inside, and grab what I need before they come back.

As it is, I barely make it before the floodlights turn on, bathing the spot where I'd been standing in bright fluorescent light.

Heart pounding, I slide between two hedges and try to slow my breathing.

My hands shake, but I clench them into fists, tightly enough to cut off circulation. Tightly enough to bruise. Tightly like I used to hold on to Brooks—

Move.

I pop out of the hedges, cursing internally when the leaves rustle.

It's not a breezy night. There isn't a lot of sound to disguise my movements.

I don't stop, though. Just continue moving until I reach the shadows of the fountain and gazebo. Only then do I breathe. The cameras are focused on the entrance and exit of the maze I'm currently navigating. I can take a second, catch my breath, allow my eyes to adjust to the growing darkness.

There.

Another gap in the hedges, just wide enough for me to squeeze through.

I suck in another silent breath.

Release it.

Move.

This one is tighter, and I have to inch my way through, holding my breath at every rustle, every branch, every crackle of a leaf.

But then I'm out.

And my quarry is just ahead, the French doors of the office dark, hiding the interior of a space I know is painted a rich blue and filled with deep brown, buttery-soft leather furniture and a huge glass and mahogany desk, its gleaming surface always somehow completely free of fingerprints.

Even though Brooks isn't one of those men who pretends to work.

He *works.*

Hard.

That was never in doubt.

Only, the man has to sleep sometime.

Hence why it's two o'clock in the morning and I'm making my approach.

He'll be in bed and—

I glance at my watch, realize I've nearly missed the next interval and burst forward out of the shadows of the hedges, sprinting for the huge potted palms that adorn either side of the entrance.

Not approaching the door—that will be watched on the cameras.

But instead, I move toward the trio of windows on one shadowed wall.

Ivy crawls up the old wooden frames, the glass clear

enough that I can see inside, see the shadows of the leather furniture, of the...desk.

I left prints there—from my fingers, my palms, my...ass.

Prints that were cleaned off within the hour.

As though I hadn't existed. As if what I experienced hadn't happened.

A familiar feeling.

Pushing that aside, I tug my picks from my pocket and study the metal latches. There are sensors on the windows, but I know the one on the right swells during the summer, the heat wreaking havoc with the old wood.

The sensor is there, but the contact plate was removed long ago.

That's my way in.

I eye the lock near the latch then select the correct pick from my set, pull out my tension wrench.

Ten seconds later, the pins in the lock have been shifted, the latch opened, and I'm sliding open the heavy sash. I haul myself in, stash away my tools, and close the window almost all the way.

My muscles are screaming from having to drag myself through the opening and my heart pounds, bile rising in my throat. Not from the exertion.

But from being here...in this room, in this place.

It's just another scene in the nightmare that became my life.

But I don't have time for this—for a mental breakdown, for a trip down memory lane. I need to get what I came for. Then I need to get the hell out and not look back.

Never look back.

Blowing out a silent breath, I take stock of the office.

It's exactly the same, with the exception of the books on the shelves lining the far wall.

My breath catches, pulse speeding further.

He doesn't read—hasn't since the moment he got his degree. He had to force himself through too many dry tomes during his college years to ever find joy in it again...or at least, that's what he always told me.

So seeing those shelves filled with books instead of refined masculine decor is such a dramatic change that I actually take a step in that direction, wanting to discover what the titles are.

Until I remember myself.

Focus.

Deliberately turning away, I shift behind the desk, ignoring the hint of his cologne—*that* hasn't changed. The scent settles heavy on my senses as I feel for the hidden latch.

It's been a long time and I only saw him do it a handful of times, so it isn't easy—

Click.

The painting behind the desk slides to the side, exposing a steel safe, the black handle basically just shadows in the darkness of the office. But next to it is a silver keypad, the gleam of LEDs nearly blinding.

Throat working, I rise on tiptoe, recall the series of numbers he didn't bother to hide from me, and begin punching them in.

It's been years.

It's likely this won't work, that all of this prep and waiting and sneaking will be for naught.

That the code has been changed and—

Two-six-nine-five. Enter.

The lights on the keypad turn green and there's a soft click.

"Holy shit," I whisper and reach for the handle...

Right as an arm winds tightly around my middle and yanks me back against a hard, strong chest.

And I hear Brooks growl,

"What the fuck do you think you're doing?"

THREE

BROOKS

SHE FREEZES.

Then the woman darts out a hand, reaching for the handle of the safe.

Caught and still trying to go for whatever she wanted to steal.

Fucking ballsy.

Or maybe fucking *stupid*.

Growling, I yank her back more firmly against me, ignoring the odd sensation that I've held her just like this before, that I've felt the lush curve of her ass brushing against my pelvis, that I've wrestled with her stubbornness.

I spin her away from the safe, shove her toward the far side of the room.

I don't know why I don't call out. Security could be here in ten seconds, could take care of this tiny woman and discover what she'd been trying to steal—and do it all faster and more efficiently than I can.

My specialty is finance.

Not interrogation.

But I don't open my mouth, don't call down the hall.

Instead, I drag her across the room and toss her on the couch.

She immediately bursts up to her feet and lurches toward the window.

A window she somehow knew wouldn't alarm when she broke in.

That pings around my brain, raising the hairs on my nape, but I don't have time to truly process that realization.

Not when she's reached the window, is yanking up the frame.

I grab her arm.

"Fuck!" I growl when her elbow digs into my side, sending pain radiating through my ribs, and she slips free, grabbing at the window again. I grind my teeth together, ignore my aching torso, and grab her before she can crawl out, gripping both of her shoulders from behind.

"Stop," I grit out, pulling her back.

She struggles against me, but I just wrap my arm around her middle and turn us, pinning her body between mine and the wall.

We're both breathing heavy and maybe I'm a fucking creep, but that lush ass is brushing against my pelvis again and my dick is getting hard and...

I grunt when she kicks back, boot scraping against my shin, slamming against my bare foot.

I lean more heavily against her. "I said *stop*."

But she doesn't stop, doesn't quit fighting, elbows jabbing into my side, boots still kicking, gloved hands trying to dislodge mine.

I should grab her more tightly—I know it. I should call out for security—I know that too.

But something inside me is unable to make that happen, unable to dig my fingers into her flesh with the intent to hurt, unable to use the force necessary to contain her, unable to call out and leave her to the men who've been paid to protect me and will have absolutely no qualms about doing what they need to in order to keep drawing a paycheck.

"Stop," I order again, the word a rasp that tangles with her staccato breathing...

And has absolutely no effect on her fight.

She has to be exhausted—I can already feel the fatigue creeping into my limbs and my lungs are working overtime, my breaths short and sharp—but she's not showing any sign of slowing down.

"Fucking *stop*," I growl. "I don't want to hurt you."

She goes still—statue still, not a single flicker of movement, not a ragged breath.

Just...*still*.

Completely still.

Yet even as I process that, she's suddenly moving again, and if I thought she was fighting before, that was child's play.

She's like a rabid dog suddenly cornered and on the offensive.

Crack!

I groan and stumble away from her when she throws her head back, her skull colliding with my chin.

Pain explodes through my face and my vision goes hazy, stars flashing and melding with the shadows of the room.

"Fuck," I groan, hands slipping from her shoulders, one lifting to my temple, the other flailing after her as she spins toward the window again.

I manage to catch the back of her knit cap, but it just slides off her head, and then my vision is hazy for a completely different reason.

Because the hair...

The *color* of that hair—

It's moonlight. Its silver shadows coaxed from the night sky. It's—

I don't even see the blow, she moves so fast, that cape of silken pearls flowing behind her as she pivots and kicks me right in the junk.

Gasping, I bend forward, hands cupped over my dick, pain a persistent and growing drumbeat through my body. Still, I reach for her again...

And slip on a sheaf of papers that must have fallen to the floor.

My arms windmill and I stagger, trying to regain my balance.

It's too late, I'm falling backward and—

Crack!

My head hits the edge of my desk and I go down hard, liquid dripping down my face.

Did I spill a drink when I fell?

No, I realize as the scent of iron hits my nose.

It's blood.

Her boots stomping on my toes, colliding with my dick hurt like a motherfucker.

Now the pain barely registers as stars and shadows fight for control of my eyesight.

There's a blip of quiet, then she whispers, "Shit," and suddenly there are hands on my face, pressing something—the beanie—against my skin. "Keep the pressure there."

Shouts ring out somewhere in the distance and she curses again.

Then she's stepping over my prone body, her footsteps clipping across the floor as she rushes away from me—

But she's not moving toward the window.

She's heading for the safe.

I hear the distinct *beep-beep-beep-beep* as she inputs the code again.

Hear the *whir* of the lock disengaging.

The scrape of the door opening.

A moment later the footsteps are coming back toward me. I groan, try to lift up so I can grab her, but she just sidesteps my hand, moves to the window, and yanks it up.

Then pauses, looks back at me.

The last thing I see before the blackness in my vision swells up and takes over...

Is a ghost with silver hair.

FOUR

BRIAR

I DON'T RELAX until after I've made the drop and I'm inside the shitty motel room hours from the grand mansion hidden among rolling hills that was supposed to be my happily-ever-after.

My knees give way and I sink to the floor, my back against the door.

I changed after I left the flash drive at the drop point—and not just my clothes.

I'd dumped the piece of shit car I bought for two hundred bucks off Facebook marketplace on a secluded roadway after changing and ditching my clothes in three separate public garbage bins.

Except my boots.

Those are too valuable to trash.

Too expensive.

Too—

I lean forward and examine the smudge that's oddly shiny

and flecking off of the black leather, then lick the pad of my thumb and rub until it's gone.

But when I start to shove my hand through my hair, the locks tickling my face, I catch sight of my thumb.

It's stained a deep coppery red.

Bile burns up the back of my throat and I lurch to my feet, rushing across the shag carpet and barely making it into the bathroom before I throw up.

Hardly anything comes up, but that's not a surprise.

I don't eat much anymore.

Just enough to sustain my body—and sometimes, when things are really tough, not even that much.

Food is expensive.

Food is an experience.

I close my eyes at the sound of Brooks's voice in my head, at the memory that brings only pain now.

And guilt.

Or maybe that's because I just cleaned his blood off my boot.

I gag again, chest heaving but nothing further comes up. Not that my body seems to understand that, the retching taking long minutes to calm.

Finally, out of breath and my throat burning, I rest my forehead against the cool porcelain, not moving until my pulse has steadied and my stomach settled.

Only then do I push up to my feet and move to the sink, scrabbling with the cardboard box that houses the tiny bar of soap, trying to ignore the flashes of red out of the corners of my eye. Then the soap is free and I wrench on the hot water, shoving my hands under the stream, lathering until bubbles are covering my skin, hiding the copper stain...and then making it disappear, swirling down the scarred basin, disappearing into the scuffed silver drain.

I watch as the red turns to pink and eventually the water runs clear.

Or that faint soapy white color, anyway.

But I still can't stop myself from keeping my hands under the water, not until it truly is clear, not the hint of a sud in sight.

That's when I finally realize that steam is clinging to my hair, my face...

And that my hand hurts.

Gasping, I pull back, wincing at the bright red of my skin then carefully turn off the water, trying to push the sight of Brooks's blood on my skin out of my brain.

He hurt me.

Guilt ripples through my body, turning my already shaky legs heavy and weak.

I could lie and say I didn't want to hurt him—not like that. Not physically, not getting violent.

I've experienced a lot of violence in my life.

Too much, I know.

But I was never the aggressor, never a person to dish out pain just because. Escaping fists and pain? Sure. I'd done a lot to get away from it, had punched and scratched and kicked and screamed until I was free.

That wasn't what happened in that dark, shadowed office.

No, that was me wanting to hurt Brooks.

I don't want to hurt you.

A lie.

A huge gaping lie.

He hurt me deeper than anyone in my life ever had— deeper than my parents who dumped me with a grandfather who didn't give two shits about me, whose only act of kindness was to not kick me out until I turned eighteen.

I had to earn my keep from the moment my parents

screeched out of his gravel driveway so fast the rocks they kicked up left me bloodied.

And scarred.

I look in the mirror, touch the faint white line at my temple.

Brooks hurt me more than them leaving, hurt me more than a surrogate parental figure making me get up before dawn to work the farm and keeping me working until well after the sun went down.

At six years old.

He hurt me more than the loneliness that was those years, six to eighteen, living on the isolated farm, rarely talking to anyone, including my paternal grandfather.

No friends.

No real family.

No soft-hearted teachers to take me under their wings.

School was a stack of books left on the kitchen table—the mix of fiction and nonfiction tomes were all I had of history and English and social studies. Math came from watching my grandfather manage the farm's finances.

After the day's work was done, of course.

After I cooked and cleaned, repaired fences and rode horses. After I dealt with snakes and patched up cattle with rudimentary animal husbandry skills. Once, I even shot at a mountain lion who was stalking our calves.

I missed, but it worked.

He or she didn't come back for another hunt.

There were long rides to wrangle loose heifers, broken bones and bloodied noses from panicked calves who didn't want to be separated from their mamas. There was bread made from scratch daily for my grandfather's breakfast, sliced and toasted and paired with eggs gathered from the coop and fried, laid out precisely next to slices of bacon or ham from pigs I cared for and named...and then had to turn into a meal.

There were bales of hay to be dragged so the animals could have breakfast even before I did. And there were chickens to be slaughtered for meals, horses to be groomed—the work never ended.

Some might say it was good for me—that it gave me a purpose and taught me many skills.

They're right.

And they're wrong.

Because John Dulvaney wasn't a good man. And neither were his friends.

There were many times a fist was used instead of firm words, many times I had to escape grasping hands and inappropriate touches and leering looks.

Many more times that shouting and insults overwhelmed quiet admonishments.

Kind words didn't happen—and neither did birthdays or Christmas or Halloween or Easter.

Those were just another day in a long line of days.

It's no wonder that I was so taken in by Brooks.

No one had ever shown me a lick of kindness and suddenly I was safe and protected and held close and spoiled.

Once he earned my trust—something he did with persistent, gentle confidence—I was lost.

He was so deep in my heart, my soul, it seemed as though I had never taken a full breath until he was standing at my back, telling me that everything would be all right.

It was so much more than *all right*.

It was a tutor so I could round out my education, it was space I could call my own. It was getting lost in books without having to worry about being up before the sun. It was gentle hands and patience and never having to worry about there being food in the kitchen.

It was a dream.

A fantasy.

Everything I never allowed myself to believe I could have.

And then it was gone.

So yeah, tonight I wanted to hurt Brooks Saxton, wanted him to hurt as much as I had these last years, to suffer as I had...

And *that* was what had me hurting him.

Not fear for myself. Not an attempt at escape.

Rage. Revenge. Venom.

Bile crawls up my throat again and it's not just the guilt I feel for my actions.

It's the look on my face as I stare at my reflection in the mirror, the anger and the frost-filled eyes and the expression that should have belonged to my grandfather looking back at me.

I promised myself.

Fucking *promised* from the moment I got out that I would be better than him, that my past wouldn't make me the person I am today.

Yet here I am, reacting with violence, cold determination settling over my bones like a familiar blanket as I shove down any bit of lingering guilt.

I hoped for better, wished for more.

And what did that get me?

Nothing.

Absolutely nothing.

My phone buzzes and I exhale, steadying myself before I pick it up and glance at the screen.

Another job.

This time, thankfully, one that has nothing to do with my past.

I type out my reply, tell them to send me the specifics.

Then I turn the shower to scorching...

And I scrub myself under the steaming hot stream until my entire body is as pink and painful as my hand.

FIVE

BROOKS

"WHAT THE FUCK HAPPENED TO YOU?" Jace mutters as he drops down into the chair next to mine.

"Dropped my phone on my face when I was doomscrolling on the couch," I say, repeating the lie I've uttered on repeat since I woke up on the floor of my study, the only evidence of the woman who left me barely conscious, the black knit cap still clutched in my hand.

Well that, and the missing flash drive.

And a raging headache that still pounds at my temples.

But when I came to, the window was closed and my security hadn't noted anything unusual—something I'm sure my lie to them didn't help with.

They didn't know they needed to be searching the shadows of the footage from the property's cameras for a tiny waif of a woman with silver hair.

Hair that—

Jace's brows come up, eyes studying mine. Then his mouth

twitches at the corners. "Almost had me." He leans close, voice dropping so it won't be overheard by those milling around the charity dinner we're both attending. "What really happened?"

"Not doomscrolling," I mutter. "But I can't talk about it here."

I'm not dumb enough to ignore that I need to tell someone what happened, and that Jace—who was there that day years ago and afterward—would understand precisely why I needed privacy for the conversation.

"Drink at my place later?" he offers.

"Marie going to be there?"

I like his wife but I'm not sure I'm ready for anyone else to know what's happening.

"No." He scowls as he leans back in his chair. "She's with Jean-Michel in Germany."

"Problem at that new site?"

Jean-Michel Dubois is one of the most powerful men in the world—he owns the vineyard we're currently sitting in, his influence so vast that the seats are full, even though he's not here to attend the fundraiser for his daughter's charity. He's also in biotech, owns a hockey team, and is a venture capitalist, along with having his own philanthropic interests.

I have more money than I could spend in a lifetime, and Jace isn't far behind me...

But we're leaps and bounds behind Jean-Michel.

Something I'm glad for. The power he wields, the fact that he's managed to use it for good, supporting smaller businesses with products that actually help people while also giving millions upon millions away each year, not to mention the responsibility he shoulders for his many employees and business ventures and charities and—

My throat closes, just the slightest bit, as panic crawls up the back of my throat.

I don't want that.

I never even wanted as much as I have now.

I just wanted to be free to love—

"Yeah," he mutters. "But she'll be home tomorrow." His mouth kicks up. "Mostly because my woman is a badass."

He's not wrong.

Marie Henderson, née Austen, began her career as Jean-Michel's assistant.

Now she's one of his most trusted associates and business partners, an absolute beast in the boardroom and fucking perfect for my friend.

Especially since he got his head out of his ass about her.

Now they're living in wedded bliss and my friend is happy.

I'm glad. He deserves it.

Even if I'm jealous.

Because I had to give all of that up in order to—

"Hi."

It's one word, but even before I turn around to see the woman who's said it, I feel my temper begin to fray.

Bailey had been a mistake.

A big one.

And even though the night I spent with her was months ago and ended without us so much as kissing, she seems to have an uncanny ability to track me down.

Running into me by chance at the gym—though I put mental quotes around the "by chance" part.

Just so happening to be grabbing a coffee around the corner from my apartment building.

Showing up in the lobby of my office—an office that I'm rarely in because I only just moved back to the Bay Area and mostly work from home.

A home that was infiltrated by a tiny, curvy woman with hair like—

Bailey settles her hand on my shoulder and steps close, the cloud of her perfume wafting forward and choking me.

Jace's nose wrinkles but he doesn't otherwise comment.

"Are you busy tonight after this?" she asks, coming closer still, pressing her body against my side...then infinitesimally parting her legs.

A small, silent message.

But a message nonetheless.

We could go home together...and I could finish the night pretending to have an orgasm.

I brush her hand off, standing in the process because even though I want naked time with Bailey like I want hot slivers shoved under my fingernails, there's a vulnerability that lingers under the surface of her sex kitten facade.

I don't want to hurt her.

I've hurt too many people, too many *women* in my life.

Silver hair. A white dress.

Lightning flashing. Thunder booming.

Rain pouring from the sky but it was her tears that were sliding down her cheeks.

"What happened to your face?" Bailey asks, coming even closer, her hands settling on my chest, her body flush with mine. "Oh, my God! It looks awful!"

"Thanks," I say dryly, grasping her wrists and gently setting her away from me. "I have plans tonight."

"Oh." Disappointment rippling through her expression. "I didn't mean to insult—"

My mouth hitches up. "You didn't."

"Good." She leans closer. "So tomorrow then?"

"Bailey," I begin.

There's that disappointment again—and it's more intense now. "Right. I get it." A shrug. "Another time maybe."

"No," I say as gently as I can. "Not another time either."

Deep blue eyes on mine, that disappointment growing until it's replaced with resignation, the vulnerable buried. "Right," she whispers. "Bye."

She turns on her heel, hair fanning out behind her—

Moonlight and shadows and silver strands dancing over my naked skin.

I blink, shove that away, and watch as she hurries from the room, her heels clicking on the winery's hardwood floor.

Most of me is relieved.

Part of me feels guilty.

Luckily, I know how to live with it.

Know how to ignore the jabs of pain, the barbed weights clinging to my insides, the regrets that slice again and again and *again.*

"Fuck, man," Jace mutters, and I shake myself, drop back into my chair.

"Yeah, you can say that again."

SIX

BRIAR

I HATE THIS.

I wish I could leave all of it behind.

But they would find me.

I know.

I've tried to leave—more than once.

And it doesn't matter how far I go, what color I dye my hair, the disguises I wear or how off the grid I try to live...they always find me.

The first time they dragged me back, they left a finger on my bathroom counter.

It wasn't mine.

It had belonged to Sylvie.

We'd become sort of friends, talked about finding our way out, starting over somewhere very far away. We even made plans to get out together.

Then she didn't show up at our meeting point...

But *they* had.

And the finger...

I sigh. I never saw her again.

The second time, I was more careful. I didn't share my plans with anyone. And I had a few weeks of peace and freedom.

Until they found me.

That's how I got the scar on my stomach. The burn marks on my back. My arm. My legs.

And the last time...well they had nearly killed me, and what they forced me to do in recompense—

I shudder.

At least like this, I can avoid the worst of the jobs, can pretend I have a modicum of freedom, can have my apartment and my books and food in the fridge and TV shows on repeat and—

My phone buzzes.

And my reality intrudes—that modicum of freedom *is* small after all...and a facsimile, able to be snatched away at any moment.

If I stop doing what they want—

Another buzz has me moving, pulling my phone out and peering down at the screen.

A change in plans.

"Shit," I whisper as I scan the text, my mind running through the consequences in rapid succession.

All of my work over the last few days goes up in smoke in an instant.

I need new clothes, need to do something about my hair—it still looks like I hacked it off with a chainsaw and I'm not going to get away with wearing a beanie or baseball hat.

I need a wig.

Then I need to conduct at least a bit of reconnaissance, exits and entrances, hiding places, getaway routes, a surefire way to slip in that won't cause suspicion and I have less than an hour to do it.

I want to whine and stomp my feet in protest, want to curse and rage at this being my life.

But I don't have time.

I need to make my exit and do it without raising any red flags.

I tug down the brim of my hat, slink toward the shadows, and wind my way through the thankfully busy lobby of the office building.

Genen-core is in biotech and though I didn't have time to do more than get the highlights, I know that Jace Henderson is the CEO, that it's one of the fastest growing companies in the US, and that I'm supposed to be inconspicuous in the lobby, waiting for the sign that the package has been dropped off.

Then I need to retrieve it without arousing suspicion and pass it off.

But the location has changed.

Hell, it *all* has changed.

My phone buzzes again with an incoming call the moment I step outside.

(See? They're always watching).

"Hello?" I answer as I hurry to my car.

"You'll need to locate Christina Dawson's office," the cold voice on the other end says, ice all but crawling through my phone's speakers as I listen to my newest orders. "She runs an animal charity."

I frown.

That doesn't seem to fit our normal modus operandi.

"Her father owns Oak Ridge vineyards, where the fundraiser will be held this evening. Jean-Michel"—my eyes flare as I place the names, mostly because everyone knows how powerful Jean-Michel Dubois is—"will no doubt have security in place, but we'll get you in through the temp agency that's supplying workers for the event tonight."

"Is he the target?"

"No. Christina is."

My frown deepens because none of this feels right. "And what happens to her?"

"She's about to have a really bad night."

"I—"

"The drive is in your car," the voice says, clearly having run out of patience. "Just download the files to her laptop and get out. They'll be too busy dealing with the shitstorm that follows to worry about anything that's happening with us."

"But—"

A deadly pause. "Do we need to have another conversation about your attitude?"

My ribs throb in memory. "No," I say quietly. "I'll get it done."

I'll frame Christina Dawson.

Who runs an animal charity.

Hanging up, I close my eyes, guilt rippling through me.

It's always the people with the softest hearts who pay first.

For a second, I consider throwing the drive away or deliber-ately making it so I get caught. It's just...

What's the point?

The family will just send someone else out to finish the job and Christina will be fucked anyway.

And it's not like the Lyons will care if I go to jail or get hurt or disappear (so long as that's permanently from this planet rather than me trying to escape so I can have a better life).

I'm disposable.

Only here to be used and then discarded when my useful-ness is used up.

Part of me wants to allow that to happen, to just end this.

I'm so damned tired.

The rest of me...well, however stupid it is, I'm making plans to get out.

I don't know how that will work yet—and maybe it *will* end with a permanently-from-this-planet sort of resolution—but I haven't completely given up.

Because maybe the tiny sliver of hope inside me—still soft and green and *alive*—is there for a reason.

Maybe I *will* find a way out.

But first I have to not get dead doing this job.

I make it to my car without issue and take an extra-long way to the winery, parking in a mostly filled row that gives me good sight lines to the back of the large, stone-covered building that overlooks the vineyard's rolling hills.

Rolling hills.

The bite of the memory is sharp, as is the guilt.

I shake my head and start up my car, having seen enough to form a plan, or the skeleton of one.

There will be no blood today. No fighting.

Just stealth and a quick in-and-out.

Why does that feel like...famous last words?

Shaking it off, I drive back through the winding roads, make a quick stop at a discount store for the necessary supplies, and then I'm securing my wig, buttoning up the bland, white collared shirt, the plain black polyester slacks. They'll do the job, but between the wig and the pants I better not get too close to any open flames, otherwise I'll be going up in a flash.

Since there are no acceptable shoes, I'm sticking with my boots, but I use a black marker to touch up the dings and scratches.

Not perfect.

Nothing about this is.

But, just like the rest of my life, I'll get through it.

I always do.

Then I'm leaving the gas station bathroom, getting in my car and driving back up to the vineyard.

This time I pull behind the building, parking among the beat-up Toyotas and the older-model Fords instead of the Range Rovers and Mercedes and Rivians. I cut the engine, allow myself just a moment to focus, to steady my nerves, then I pop the door, get out, and follow the stream of similarly clad workers into the building.

A brunette with striking blue eyes is standing in the kitchen, smiling at us as we file in to fill the small room.

I stand awkwardly in the corner, waiting for orders, but to my surprise the woman comes close to us, her smile only growing.

"Thank you in advance for your work tonight. My charity couldn't exist without you and while I know this is likely just another job for you, the animals you're helping really appreciate it. As do I."

Something happens in my heart, my belly—the sliver of hope growing, the kernel of hate getting just a little smaller.

There's something so genuinely sweet and earnest about this woman, and I can't help but like her. "Please make sure you eat at some point tonight," she says. "We have food available now and the kitchen will make sure you'll have options as well to take home after the event. And if you like wine"—a nod to a table positioned on the far wall—"there are two bottles there for each of you." Her mouth kicks up. "And please don't forget to grab one of the goodie bags on your way out. I promise if you use the bath salts, your feet and body will thank you tomorrow."

She waves and smiles again then slips out of the room, leaving a pair of woman with clipboards to take over.

"Is she for real?" I find myself whispering as we line up.

A slender blonde turns to me. "First time?"

I nod, even as I'm kicking myself for drawing attention. I'm going for stealth, for a quick in-and-out.

Small talk isn't part of that.

"Yeah," I say because I have to say *something*.

"Chrissy is great," the blonde tells me. "She wants to raise money for her charity, but she also actually cares about us. We're not just interchangeable robots to her." She leans close, rubs her fingers together. "And if you stick around to the very end, she'll make her gratitude known in cold hard cash."

Chrissy who runs a charity.

The slender thread of hope inside me dies a quick death.

Because what are the chances that she's Christina Dawson née Dubois who *owns* the charity putting on this fundraiser?

The Christina I'm supposed to frame for a crime from tonight.

SEVEN

BROOKS

"I'M GOING to head home and change," I tell Jace. "We drinking at my place or yours?"

"Yours," Jace says with a smirk. "I'm not risking the wrath of Marie."

"We're not college kids on a bender."

"Those bruises on your face say otherwise." Before I can retort, someone calls out his name and he turns, lifts a hand in greeting. Then he glances over at me with a sigh. "I need to make the rounds here for a little while longer, but I'll meet you at your apartment. I'll bring the pizza, you pick up the bourbon."

Bender indeed.

It doesn't get any closer to college blackout antics than pizza and alcohol.

Probably for the best we're doing this at my place.

Especially since although the food served tonight was delicious, there wasn't a lot of it to go around. Jean-Michel's award-winning Oak Ridge Petite Sirah was flowing freely, along with champagne from his vineyard in France and Pinot Grigio from Italy.

Not a surprise.

Tipsy people donate more.

"That's a deal," I say, shaking Jace's hand and hitching my head to the side. "I'll give Chrissy my regards then I'm out."

"Try not to fall asleep before I get there, old man."

"Cute," I mutter.

"Hey"—a shrug—"I'm not the one who's a whole year older."

"For the record, it's only ten months."

He grins. "Ten months closer to the end, you mean."

I roll my eyes. "Why did I come back here again?"

"Because you missed me." He shoves my shoulder. "Now go home and turn on the hockey game. I'll be right behind you."

Right behind me.

Sure.

He'll probably get distracted and then I won't get any pizza.

Or bourbon.

That's why I call an audible. "I'll pick up the pizza," I tell him. "You bring the alcohol."

If worse comes to worst, I have beer in my fridge and my college-esque bender will be covered.

And maybe if I drink the beer *and* the bourbon I'll forget about hair the color of moonlight and a boot connecting with my junk and a missing flash drive with information that threatens to undo the very roots of my company.

"Don't eat it all," Jace says.

"No promises," I mutter.

He shoves my shoulder. "Asshole."

I shrug.

He's not wrong.

Something he obviously knows because he just snorts and turns away, heading toward the couple who flagged him down a few minutes ago.

He's quickly drawn into what looks like a pretty serious conversation, and I don't delay further, just down the rest of my glass of wine, set it on an empty tray, and then head for the exit.

Unfortunately, it's not a clean getaway.

Though at least this time I'm not waylaid by the perfume cloud known as Bailey.

"Brooks Saxton as I live and breathe."

Nope.

It's worse.

Summer Sandringham is about as high society as one gets in the Bay Area filled with tech magnates and Hollywood transplants.

Mrs. Sandringham is, unfortunately, both of those things— her family founded and continues to head one of the biggest film production companies in the world and her husbands (yes, plural *husbands* because she buried two, divorced one, and is finally quote-unquote happily married to a fourth) all either owned, were on the boards of, or started multi-billion-dollar dot coms.

She's a force of nature.

And there's no way I can just brush her off.

Not even if pizza is calling.

"Hi, Mrs. Sandringham, how are you?"

"Summer, please." She smooths a hand down my chest. "And I'll call you Brooks."

I catch her fingers, bring them up to my lips, ignoring the little titter she gives and the fact that the gesture gives me the creeps. I've got to give her something.

Otherwise she'll get even handsier.

And seriously, happily married? Yeah, I'm still waiting for evidence on that front.

"What can I do for you?" I ask, knowing that she hasn't stopped me to discuss the weather.

"What are you doing Monday morning at ten-thirty?"

"Working," I reply honestly.

"At your downtown office?"

It's impossible to miss the calculation in her eyes.

Still, what am I going to say?

"More than likely," I hedge.

"Great. I'll see you then."

"I—" I blink, mouth falling open. Then she's leaning in, lips parting, getting so close I can see the faint wrinkles at the corners, the way the lipstick's begun to wear off in the middle, the slightly *off* color of one of her bottom teeth. "Excuse me?"

She pecks my cheek then pulls back, patting the other one. "You're excused." She turns away, tossing over her shoulder, "See you Monday!"

She melts into the crowd and all I can do is stare after her.

"Now if that's not the look of a man who's just been befuddled by one Summer Sandringham, I'll eat my hat."

Turning, I smile at Chrissy, Jean-Michel's daughter, and a woman who's left many a man befuddled herself. "Summer strikes again."

A wince. "I'm sorry about that. She's a lot, but she's supported the charity a lot over the years."

"*A lot* is the right description for her." I touch Chrissy's shoulder. "And she's fine. A little handsy but otherwise harmless."

"Handsy?" Concern ripples across her face.

Shit.

"It's fine," I say. "I promise. Look," I add before she can

delve too deep into that, "I wanted to see you before I left. Is there someplace we can talk privately?"

Striking blue eyes on mine—and it has to be said that she has her father's ability to use those eyes to pierce straight into souls.

Then she inclines her head and leads me from the room, down a corridor, eventually pausing outside a door. "My dad's office," she says before adding with a smile, "On the very rare occasions he works inside and not out in the vineyard."

Jean-Michel Dubois—billionaire, hockey team owner, philanthropist, and complete and utter wine enthusiast, from grape selection to planting all the way up to uncorking the delicious stuff. Once, I took a meeting with him while he was fixing a tractor...he talked contract terms and then showed me how to repair a hydraulic leak.

No surprise the office is all but bare.

Except for a laptop, a coat hanging on the back of the door, and what looks like a pair of slippers and pajamas propped on a chair.

"After party comfy clothes," Chrissy explains, clearly following my gaze. "A must after an event like this."

My lips twitch. "I bet." I lean back against the wall. "Speaking of events..."

"It was really nice of you to attend." Her words come in a rush when I pause, trying to sort how to phrase what I need to say next. "I know you're busy, but you being so generous with your time—and your silent auction item—really means a lot."

"About that—"

"We've opened a new adoption center and we're expanding our support services to other counties." Her eyes light up. "My hope is that we'll create a system that covers the entire state, and maybe, one day we'll be able to help animals all across the country and..."

Her passion is a beautiful thing.

So fucking beautiful it takes my breath away, steals my words, reminds me of another time, another woman who wanted to help.

A piece of my soul I tore off and walked away from.

A ghost from my past I couldn't allow myself to have.

And because of that passion, I can't turn away.

I can't do anything but stand here and listen to Chrissy Dawson talk about her plans for the future.

The same as I couldn't do anything but stand transfixed when Briar first spoke to me all those years before.

EIGHT

BRIAR

I PULLED the whole I-forgot-something-in-my-car-I'll-be-right-back to give myself a moment to breathe.

To calm down.

To bury the guilt that continues to slip out from behind my shield, slashing at my insides.

But as the sun began to set, turning the horizon into a rainbow, I managed to contain my feelings.

Sure Chrissy seems nice and she puts on a good front about caring for the people who are schlepping food and drinks for her, but she's just like the rest of them.

And we're interchangeable, disposable.

Meaningless.

On that lovely thought, I make my way inside just in time to come face-to-face with the lady with the clipboard.

"Name?" she asks sharply.

"Sorry," I say, "I just had to run out because I left my phone in my car."

Her gaze lifts from the clipboard, one eyebrow lifting.

In judgment.

Shit.

Because I'm supposed to be working and not on my phone.

"Don't worry," I tell her quickly, shoving it into my purse. "I'm not planning on using it. I just didn't want to leave it out in the open."

The eyebrow slides back down. "Name?" she says again and it's not exactly warm and fluffy, but at least it's not edged with ice.

And damn, I should have been using this time to come up with a name.

Except, it's not going to be on that clipboard.

Which means she won't let me inside. I can see that on her face, see it in the firm lines of her expression, her brow slowly arching up again.

I open my mouth...

Just as I'm shoved from behind, hard enough that I topple into the woman, her clipboard smacking me in the face as I fall onto my hands and knees.

Pain flames through my kneecaps, my palms.

"Oh, my God!" I hear. "What is wrong with you?"

"Sorry, I didn't see you there."

I glance over my shoulder, spot a delivery guy carrying a huge box in front of him.

"Why are you coming in this way?" she snaps. "We take deliveries at the other door."

"What do you mean? I always bring them here—"

A scoff. "Certainly not."

The clipboard is right there and I don't waste any more time—though I can't deny it crosses my mind that this is a setup, a way for me to get past Clipboard Lady without blowing my cover.

Always watching.

They're *always* watching.

I shiver, the hairs on my nape lifting, as though those eyes are on me, even now.

And they probably are.

I pick up the clipboard, scanning rapidly as she gets rid of the delivery guy, getting to my feet just as a hand lands on my arm.

I flinch, pull away.

I wish I didn't. Wish that instinct wasn't there, that I could bury it because it reveals too much.

But...

I don't, or I'm not able to, or—

"Sorry," Clipboard Lady says and there's definitely no ice in her tone now. It's gentle, almost conciliatory.

"It's okay," I say quickly, climbing to my feet. "Are you all right?" I ask, passing her the clipboard.

A pause. "Yeah. You?"

I nod, take a breath. "My name is Rebecca." The only no-show on the list.

A no-show who would, hopefully, continue to *no* show.

Her eyes flick down and back up before she studies me for a long moment. But all she says is, "You're in the coat room."

Coat room.

I don't know what I thought that would entail aside from applying the proper use of hangers and giving out tickets.

I *do* know I've worked harder in the last couple of hours than I expected.

The coats are heavy, the ticket book has given me paper cuts left and write...er, *right*. Though, I have been doing a lot of *writing*, scribbling down the items that were checked in and out on a spreadsheet Clipboard Lady insisted we use.

Seems like overkill, but what do I know about fancy charity events?

"You should go eat."

I blink, the words that had gone blurry on the paper in front of me coming into sharp focus. "What?" I ask of my co-coat checker in crime.

"Dissociate much?" Dale asks.

I lean back against the counter as he smiles, his eyes dragging down my body and back up in a way that so totally does nothing for me.

Not like the press of Brooks's chest against my back had just a few nights ago.

Not like Brooks giving me the same look would have done years—

I shove that down. "Sorry," I say, mirroring his smile. "Yeah, I was zoning out."

He leans against the counter beside me. "The party's going to start winding down soon, which means we're going to get slammed with people and then if you're sticking around for cleanup—" He pauses and I nod.

Hopefully, I'll be long gone by then.

But it pays to be flexible.

"We'll be busy for a while yet," he says. "Though, maybe after we're done for the night, we can go out for a drink?"

I barely hold back my shudder.

"No?"

Damn. I don't like the hard edge to his tone, the way he's shifting closer, so his arm brushes against mine.

"How about I call it a maybe?" I smile and force myself to stay still, something in his eyes, his demeanor, that sharp edge of his words, telling me to tread carefully. "I'm just coming off working a couple of doubles. But," I add when his eyes narrow, "if not tonight then tomorrow?"

He studies me closely. "Give me your number."

A demand.

Yeah, this one is full of red flags left and right.

But it's a demand I can give in to—mostly because the burner phone in my pocket is getting dumped tonight.

I recite the numbers, watch as he plugs them in...and then hits the button to make a call.

My phone vibrates in my pocket.

He grins, friendly ally vibes reactivated now that he's gotten what he wants.

Yup.

So, *so* many red flags.

"I'm going to take your advice and grab something to eat," I tell him. "Want me to bring you back something?"

"Nah." A shrug. "I snagged a plate after I used the bathroom."

Hopefully, he washed his hands before getting all up in the buffet they laid out for us.

Though, that seems...unlikely.

Because red flags.

I nod and slip out of the coat-check booth. As creepy as Dale is, his suggestion is actually good timing.

It gives me some space to do what I need to do.

I slip down the hall, turn the corner, and—

Slam!

For the second time that night, I'm knocked down, pain radiating through my palms, my knees.

"Dammit," I whisper, trying to breathe through the hurt.

But I don't get that far.

Nope.

The hurt intensifies, hardening to a sharp point as a voice says, "Shoot. I'm sorry. I didn't see you there."

His hand appears in front of my face.

No. Not *his*.

Brooks's.

NINE

BROOKS

FUCK.

I feel like a dick, so in my own head, my own past that I wasn't paying attention to where I was going.

And now I've knocked the tiny, curvy brunette to the floor.

"Here," I coax, shaking my hand slightly when she doesn't move, just keeps looking at the terracotta tiles.

Nothing.

"Hey," I say, crouching down.

It's like me dropping to her level startles her into motion.

She bursts to her feet, shoulder bumping mine on the way up.

I wobble and she rushes by me, heading for the winding corridors.

My palm slams onto the floor, steadying myself, but my focus is on the woman who's all but sprinting away from me...

And the boots on her feet.

I lurch up and don't think, instinct telling me that if I don't go *now* I won't ever see her again.

I follow her as she whips around the corner, darts through a service hallway.

She's fast.

But I'm faster.

And I'm not going to be taken by surprise again.

I dodge the elbow she throws toward my gut when I get close, gripping the tops of her shoulders and pushing her against the wall. "Stop," I order when she struggles, when she kicks back at my shins.

Not a surprise, she doesn't.

But I'm stronger, and this time I don't hold back on my strength.

I won't hurt her, but I'm not letting up.

Not until I have some fucking answers.

I shuffle her toward the exit, glad we're in the quiet corridor so no one can see me all but abducting her.

Her.

Briar.

I can smell her, *feel* her, see a glimpse of that moonlight hair through the wig that's been knocked slightly askew.

Not a ghost.

Not a shadow of the past hidden in the darkness of night.

It's *her.*

I plant a hand on the door and shove it open, stepping out into the cool spring air.

Then grunt as she kicks back again.

I just tighten my grip and drag her to my car, shoving her into the passenger seat and slamming the door.

Which she tries to immediately open.

I beep the locks, round the hood, and wait until she stops

struggling before I unlock the driver's door to get in, reengaging them behind me.

I turn on the ignition.

Wait.

"Buckle up," I order.

Arms crossed, she doesn't move, just glares out the windshield.

"Briar."

Those arms cross tighter, but she continues playing a statue.

Temper fraying—and temple aching in reminder of the other night—I twist, reaching over the console.

Her flinch fucking *kills* me.

But I can't afford to let my guard down. Not now. Not here.

I keep moving, though I do it slower, reaching for the seat belt, dragging it across her chest and buckling it in place.

I straighten, trying to catch her eyes, to look into a face I once knew better than my own, but she's looking out the window now, and her body is so damned tense...

Like it had been when I first met her, when I had to carefully make my way through all of those walls.

It fucking burns, the truth of that.

I created it. I'm the reason for it.

And...it still fucking burns.

I reach for the wig, wanting it off, wanting nothing but her.

"Don't," she rasps.

I freeze, my fingers on the synthetic strands that do nothing but remind me they're fake, they're not her.

Fucking sandpaper compared to the silk of her hair.

"It's pinned in place." The words are quiet. Husky.

A thousand questions barrel through my mind, spinning like a fucking tornado, but before I can quiet the storm, can pluck a question out of the maelstrom to ask, her eyes come to mine.

They spear into me, the burning in my belly growing, expanding out and consuming my insides.

"You need to let me go and pretend you never saw me."

The words are cold...but her eyes—

Fuck, her eyes are *dead*.

I did that.

The guilt, it's so fucking heavy, sitting so deeply on my lungs that it feels impossible to draw in a breath.

She reaches for the handle.

I stay her arm.

"I can't," I rasp.

Her eyes close and then she turns her head away, but she doesn't try to get out again as I put the transmission into reverse, as I navigate the winding road down from the winery, as I take the freeway to the city, as I turn into the underground garage for my apartment building.

I park in my spot and rotate to face her.

She's still looking away from me.

"Briar."

She doesn't move.

"Raindrop—"

It slips out, and it has her eyes flashing to mine. "I *hate* you."

I shrug even though the words flay me open, regret and guilt spilling out like a defeated knight's entrails on a long-forgotten battlefield.

But I'm not a white knight.

That was the problem.

Swallowing, I pop the driver's side door, move around to hers and tug open the metal panel.

Briar doesn't move so I unbuckle her belt, wrap my fingers

around her wrist and draw her out of the car. But she doesn't fight me either.

Not as I guide her to the elevator, not as I bring her up to the penthouse.

Not as I unlock my door and she walks inside.

"Bathroom?" she asks in that cold, dead voice before I can say anything...or figure out what to say, anyway.

I nod down the hall then follow her, flicking on lights and pushing open the door when we reach the hall bath.

But when she goes to shut it, I grip the wooden panel. "No."

I expect a tart reply, something snarky about picking up a kink.

Instead, she just shakes her head and moves to the mirror, fingers sinking into the wig.

Plink. Plink. Plink.

Pins slide out of her hair, drop onto the counter.

I lean back against the doorframe, watching her, on edge for her to attack me again, for cold, dead words that slide deep. But also bleeding out.

Because I watched her like this so many times before.

Wiping off her makeup, putting shit on her face that was supposed to make her more beautiful (fucking impossible), and my favorite—taking down her hair.

Combing it with long, slow strokes, putting something in the ends that smelled incredible.

Sometimes she would let me comb it for her...

And I'd always find a way to do it with both of us naked.

The *plinks* of the pins on the counter stop and I find myself holding my breath as she reaches up again, as the wig slides free.

She sets it on the counter.

My lungs seize.

Moonlight hair.

A slender neck.

Earlobes I used to nibble at, a jaw I would press my nose to and inhale, a nose I'd kiss, staring into eyes filled with laughter.

In short, the most beautiful woman I've ever seen.

Then she undoes the tight bun, releasing those locks, and the edges of my vision go black.

TEN

BRIAR

I'M BARELY HOLDING it together, especially with him standing there.

My fingers fumble with the pins, tremble as I draw off the wig, shake when I take down the bun.

His inhale is sharp and it burns through me, through the shields I'm struggling to erect, to keep in place so I can get the fuck out of here.

If the criminal organization that now owns my life was speaking in my ear, they'd tell me to lean in to that sharp breath, to use my body to distract him so I can extricate myself from this scenario.

But that won't work.

Because he sees me now.

And even though he was the one who left me, who pushed me away, who destroyed the small slice of happiness I held—

"Don't look at me like that," I snap.

He doesn't move. "Like what?" he asks hoarsely.

"Like you miss me."

"Raindrop—"

"*Don't.*"

"I didn't want to break things off," he says. "I swear I didn't."

I snort, keep removing pins. "You could have fooled me," I mutter. "What with you leaving me at the altar and all."

"Briar." He sighs. "I left because—"

"I don't care anymore," I say, even though I do care. I care *too* fucking much.

He's quiet. "I had to leave."

"Right," I mutter then lift my chin. "I need to go."

There's a pause, long enough that my gaze is drawn back to his, and I see it, right there in his eyes.

He's not going to let me leave.

Dammit.

"Why'd you do it?"

I pause, hands dropping to my sides, hair falling forward to tickle my face. "Do what?" I hedge, even though I know exactly what he's talking about.

"Steal the flash drive."

"I had to. Same as you"—I make finger quotes—"*had* to leave me at the altar on our wedding day."

"No," he says. "I had to leave because otherwise they would have taken you."

I freeze, ice skittering down my spine. "What?"

"You know my father worked with people who were"—he shakes his head and that ice grows—"unsavory in their business practices. They didn't like that I pulled out of those shared endeavors and made it very clear what would happen to you if I didn't join forces with them again."

"What?" I ask again.

"I tried to—" He looks away. "I tried to keep you safe—tried so fucking *hard*." His voice drops to a whisper. "But, in the end, the only thing I could do was leave."

My heart thuds hard against my ribs.

"I loved you enough to let you hate me."

His words swirl around my head, too much, too fast, too many feelings threatening to escape.

He's lying.

He has to be.

This is some sort of sick joke and sooner or later, he'll get tired of fucking with me. Then he'll call the cops and I'll go to jail and this will all be over.

My eyes flick to the mirror and my reflection...

Fuck, I hate it so much.

The roughly cut hair, the dark circles beneath my eyes, the hollow cheeks, the scar near my right ear.

Not enough for him. Not enough for anyone.

Stop. Forcing myself to breathe slowly in and out, I shore up the ice around my heart, my thoughts, and glance at the toilet.

I'm here.

Might as well use it.

Might as well embrace the humiliation, the lack of power.

And hell, I'll probably be in jail in a couple of hours, so I might as well go to the bathroom in semi-privacy, right?

I unbutton my slacks, push them down, allowing them to pool onto the floor.

Out of the corner of my eye, I see him jerk. "What are you doing?"

"Using the bathroom," I mutter and turn, moving to the toilet.

He inhales again and it's only then I realize I've made a critical error.

My legs are bare and the backs of them...

"What the fuck happened to you?"

His voice is close, too close and I jump.

"Don't touch me," I snap, darting away from him.

"Baby," he rasps, dropping to his knees, hand lifting, fingers mere inches from my bare legs. I scooch back.

He can't touch me.

He *can't.*

"What happened?" he asks, his voice like gravel.

My gaze slips to his, and I know it's a mistake, know I should be slamming the lid on this, should be exploiting this so I can get away.

But the horror in his brown eyes...it pins me in place.

Sends a hairline fracture through my icy cold shields.

I can't have that.

I *can't* have it.

So, I do the only thing I can.

I tell him the truth.

"You."

I DIDN'T EXPECT him to leave.

Certainly not to do it without a word.

But the moment I finished speaking, he was on his feet and leaving the room, closing the door behind him.

I lurch toward it, flicking the lock before I start searching through the drawers for a weapon, for a way out of here.

It doesn't take long to find the can of air freshener and I set it aside before continuing my search.

Towels. Toilet paper. Soap.

No good weapons.

Search complete, I take care of business and wash my hands, pulling up my pants and retying my boots. The can fits in my pocket—barely, the bulge far too obvious, and far too challenging to pull free in a hurry. But it's all I have.

I exhale.

Then brace, patching up those spiderweb cracks, my mind turning through the possibilities, trying to find a way out of here that doesn't end up with me dead or in prison.

All that bracing, that mind spinning...

And it doesn't make the least bit of difference when I pull open the door and see him standing there.

Fuck, he's beautiful and the impact of that sends cracks skittering through me once again.

He tilts his head and pushes off the wall, uncrossing his ankles and turning in the direction of the front door.

I watch his back as he walks away from me, as he moves through the space and into the kitchen, pulling open the door of the fridge.

"It's unlocked," he calls.

I hadn't even realized I'd moved, trailing him but pausing in the intersection of hallways.

Forward leads to the open-space living room, the kitchen, and dining area. Left...leads to the front door.

"You can go."

Head jerking up at the sound of his voice suddenly so close, I see he's stopped in front of me, a bottle of water in his hands.

"But I hope you'll stay just a little while longer."

He offers up the water bottle and I take it with numb fingers.

He said those words before.

Years ago when I was considering my exits, plotting the best course of escape.

And I'd stayed. I'd listened and talked and *fell*.

In like. In lust. In *love*.

Then he'd shattered all of that without a single look back.

I take a step toward the door.

His breath is short, sharp.

But he doesn't stop me.

And for some reason...*I* stop me, hesitating in that inter-section.

I need to go. I *need* to.

Yet, my feet won't let me.

"So you can arrest me?" I probably—no, definitely *stupidly* —ask.

His mouth kicks up. "I could have done that already, don't you think?"

Maybe.

Or maybe the police are on the way. Or his crazy security company is watching us through some cleverly placed cameras, waiting for me to admit—

"Why the thumb drive?"

I clench my teeth together, look away...and unfortunately, it's right to the windows where the city's lights are twinkling beyond.

God, that's beautiful.

Like stars on the backdrop of the evening sky.

"Did you know what was on it?"

A bolt of pain shoots through my jaw and though I want to tell him I have no fucking idea, that I don't have any control over what I do or who I steal from or the incriminating photos I take or the evidence I plant.

But I can't.

He's not going to save me.

He can't help me—even if he wanted to.

So, I should go.

My stomach growls, breaking the silence that's fallen.

He doesn't say anything, just watches me for a long moment before turning and heading for the kitchen, tugging open the fridge door again, rummaging through the contents. "You still like omelets?"

My stomach rumbles again, answering for me.

So instead of getting the hell out of here like I should, I ignore the mindfuck of memories—how many nights had we snuck into the kitchen to make them?—and I follow him.

Food.

I need to keep my strength up.

Then I'll walk right out the front door.

ELEVEN

BROOKS

I HOLD my breath until I hear her footsteps start coming my way.

Then I exhale to steady my nerves...and maybe to give myself time to wonder what in the fuck all I'm doing.

She stole from me.

Hit me.

And all the reasons I walked away still exist.

But—

Scars on the back of her legs.

Flinching when I moved too fast.

The disguise tonight...

The fucking fact that she broke into my house—our house —and stole from me.

I grab the eggs, bring them to the counter, along with the cheese and bacon, green onions and mushrooms. It's instinct to gather the ingredients, to snag the right pan from the drawer beneath the stove.

I don't spend much time here—when I moved back to the States, I preferred to be at the estate. After pretending for so long that the hole inside me I created by leaving her didn't exist, all I wanted was to spend time in the place I had her. To fill that void with memories.

Good.

Until they turned bad.

The footsteps stop.

I open the carton, start cracking eggs into a bowl.

"Knife and cutting board are there and there"—I nod at the block and then a drawer—"and you're more than welcome to keep the spray you have in your pocket, but I think that a knife will be a better weapon." I shrug. "Though, those boots are pretty damned good as they are."

She doesn't move, not for a long moment.

Then she sighs quietly and moves to the drawer, pulling it open, snagging a cutting board. A moment later, she has a knife in hand.

And is turning toward me.

I can't lie. I definitely feel a blip of discomfort with that shining blade in her hand.

But she doesn't plunge the knife in my back.

She folds a towel and places it beneath the cutting board, starts slicing the mushrooms and green onions.

I scramble the eggs.

She dices the bacon, tosses it in the pan.

And then we're working like we always used to, side-by-side with crisp efficiency.

Frying the bacon, sautéing the mushrooms and onions.

Setting them aside.

Eggs in the pan. Fillings joining the party along with the cheese and salt and pepper.

Five minutes later, I'm sliding her omelet onto a plate and starting on mine.

"I don't understand," I say as I pretend to focus on the eggs in the pan, but really I'm watching her out of the corner of my eye, watching as she slowly takes a bite, chews, and swallows.

Then it's like something has unlocked inside her.

She devours the omelet, eating it as though she hasn't had a full meal in far too long—and maybe she hasn't.

Fuck, with everything that's happened, I haven't really processed that she's far too thin. Her cheekbones stand out in sharp relief, her jawline sharp—too sharp. And there's a fragility about her she never had before, not even when she first left the farm and crossed paths with the shitstorm that's my life.

I know it's not physical, the bruise on my temple tells me that much, but I still fucking hate it.

I hate you.

Right. Probably as much as she hates me.

For leaving her that day, for hurting her so deeply.

I slide my omelet onto her plate and she stills, those eyes that see too much and reveal nothing aside from disdain, glancing across mine.

Then she uses the edge of her fork to cut off a piece and pops it into her mouth.

I'm hungry but my stomach is in knots.

No way could I eat anything right now.

So I clean up, the silence only broken by the clink of her fork and the splash of water and the rattle of the pans.

Eventually there are no more dishes, nothing else to put away.

Nothing except the pressing silence, closing in on all sides, leaving me at a complete loss as what to say and do and...

"I need to go," she says, reaching into her pocket and pulling out the can of air freshener, setting it on the counter.

"Don't."

She freezes, fingers spasming on the can, but then her voice changes—for the first time losing the edge of biting frost. "I'm not going to hurt you again." Her throat works. "I didn't like..." A shake of her head. "I need to go."

"*Don't*," I rasp again.

A breath. "You have no right to ask me to stay."

That's true. I was the one who walked away, who shattered what we had and threw the pieces to the side.

"I know," I say quietly. "But stay anyway."

She shakes her head, steps back from the counter, turns for the hall.

My heart drops.

"The scars?"

A hitch in her step. "They don't matter."

"They do to me."

"Are you sure?"

Fuck. The ice is back.

The gulf between us is so fucking wide that I don't even know where to begin. I just...

"Don't go."

Another shake of her head and she starts walking again, this time moving more quickly, and I follow her.

"You broke into our house."

A pause. "Not *our*," she snaps icily. "You made that clear when you left me on that mountain five years ago."

"So you stole from me?"

Her mouth closes so quickly, the *click* of her teeth slamming together is audible. "I'll make sure you don't see me again."

But there's something in the lines of her body as she reaches for the doorknob, in the set of her jaw...

"But you can't guarantee that, can you?"

She stills. Only for a heartbeat, but it's long enough that I know.

"Why were you at our house?"

"It's not *our* house."

Because *I* made it that way.

She doesn't say it.

But I hear it.

"Did you know what you were stealing?"

"That doesn't matter."

"Doesn't it?" I shift closer. "Why that flash drive, Briar? What are you going to do with the information?"

Her fingers close around the metal of the knob.

"Are you going to sell it?"

I reach around her, place my palm flat on the door, holding it closed.

"Blackmail me with it?"

She's stiff, her words frosty. "I just told you that you wouldn't see me again."

"What if that's not what I want?"

A dumb fucking question.

I left her, made it pretty fucking clear we were finished five years ago.

She looks over her shoulder at me, and for a second, her eyes aren't filled with ice...it's like we're there again.

In the past.

Without...

All of this shit between us.

Shit I created.

"Just let me go," she whispers. "Forget I was here and we'll go back to our lives."

A life that's left her rail-thin and scarred and flinching at abrupt movements.

A life that has her stealing things and wearing disguises and carrying air freshener like it can be used as a weapon.

I open my mouth to tell her there's no fucking way I can let her walk out the door, but before I get a word out...

There's a knock on the other side of the door.

TWELVE

BRIAR

MY STOMACH TWISTS, and I curse myself for getting lost in those gorgeous brown eyes of his.

But when he goes to draw me away from the door, reaches for the knob, I grab his wrist. "No," I say, bile burning the back of my throat. "Don't open it."

The Lyons will have followed me here.

They must have.

If I were thinking clearly, I might have realized that's dumb, that of course they won't come here.

That they won't strike out now.

No. They'll wait until the precise moment to do the most damage with the least risk of exposure.

Brooks stills and I can see in his eyes that I've revealed too much.

"Yo!" I hear bellowed through the wood. "You'd better not be eating all the pizza without me."

Brooks curses.

"What?"

"It's Jace."

Jace.

Jace?

This cannot be happening.

I shake my head, lips parting to tell Brooks that under no circumstance should he open the freaking door, but he's already pulling me behind him and turning the handle and—

"What the fuck were you doing in here—?"

It would be funny—the comical way Jace's mouth drops open when he spots me standing behind Brooks—except that he's here.

And I'm here.

And Brooks is here.

Fuck, I really need to go.

"I'll let you two catch up," I say, slipping out from behind Brooks and making a beeline for the open door.

Jace blocks me, stepping forward at the same time. "Holy shit, Briar. Is that you?" He moves close, as though he's going to hug me, and...

I flinch.

Fucking *flinch.*

Too fast. Too big.

Too many times I've been hurt.

He halts almost immediately, gaze flicking toward Brooks, something unreadable crossing his face.

Then he closes the door. "What the fuck is going on?"

This is my nightmare.

My *literal* nightmare.

"I need to go."

"Why don't you tell me?"

Brooks and I speak at the same time and Jace's gaze flicks between us, as though trying to decide which of us to address.

He seems to settle on Brooks. "What are you talking about?" he asks.

"She's lost weight, eats like she hasn't had a full meal in far too long, hits hard enough to leave fucking bruises"—Jace's eyes widen—"and carries air freshener like it could be a fucking weapon—"

"It can," I blurt.

I have no freaking idea why I interject.

I need them to be distracted by each other so I can get the hell out.

Now they're both looking at me.

And I find myself repeating, "It can."

Brooks just looks at Jace.

No, he *glares* at Jace.

Who just looks at me. "How?"

"How what?"

"How can it be used as a weapon?"

I nibble at the inside of my mouth then mentally shrug, figure there's no harm in telling him. "Spray it in someone's eyes and it works fine."

Jace looks at Brooks.

I look at Brooks...and see his jaw is clenched so tightly a muscle begins to flicker in his cheek.

The silence stretches, growing so taut it threatens to snap. Then he grits out, "So, Jace—my best fucking friend—want to tell me why in the hell she looks the way she looks and acts the way she acts and is thinking about how to use air freshener as a fucking *weapon?*"

My surprise has morphed back into anger. "Why do you care? You're the one that walked away."

He glares down at me. "Then you reappear five years later, helping yourself to my safe and leaving me unconscious when I try to stop you."

That anger shatters, consumed by guilt. "I'm sorry. I..." A dozen explanations cross my mind, and I can't share any of them. "I'm just...sorry."

His glare softens. "Why did you steal it?"

I close my eyes. "I need to go."

"And *I* need that flash drive," he says and my lids fly open. "But I'm pretty sure that neither of us are going to get what we want tonight. Now"—he glances back at Jace and the sudden tension in the room has me holding my breath—"do you want to explain why in the fuck she was in a place to miss meals and learn how to use air freshener as a weapon?"

Jace's eyes drift back to mine and I know what he's going to say...

And what he's *not* going to say in order to protect me.

I settle my hand on Brooks's arm. "I didn't touch the money."

Slowly, he turns to face me. "Excuse me?"

"Jace gave me the information for the account. I refused to touch it." I take a breath. "When he insisted, I emptied the account and donated the money."

Brooks slowly turns back to Jace.

But when I go to lift my hand from his arm, his palm covers my fingers, holds it in place.

And despite how mad I am, how hurt, how much guilt I have for hurting him, warmth blooms in my chest.

Jace sighs and rubs his forehead. "I think we all need pizza and bourbon."

I'm not hungry.

I just had two giant omelets.

But my stomach doesn't get the message.

It rumbles loudly at the mention of pizza.

And God? When was the last time I had a glass of bourbon?

I can't even remember.

But it was probably with these same two men.

Jace's mouth quirks up. "I'll order the pizza and booze. Maybe get the woman a snack."

They break away as one, the fluid movements showcasing a friendship that's been built and strengthened over the years— Brooks moving to the fridge, pulling it open, and perusing the contents while Jace flicks the lock on the door, reaches into his pocket, and tugs out his phone.

But before he starts tapping on the screen, he lifts his free hand.

Slowly, like I'm a cornered animal, he cups my jaw. "It's good to see you, kid," he says gently.

I bite the inside of my cheek, blink back the burn of tears. "It's good to see you too."

He smiles and it's sad. "I just—" He cuts himself off with a shake of his head.

"You just...what?"

A sigh and he drops his hand.

"I just wish you'd taken the money, kid."

THIRTEEN

BROOKS

JACE TILTS his head toward the door, and I carefully push myself up from the couch, not wanting to disturb Briar.

She devoured a quarter of the huge pizza Jace ordered and drank two glasses of bourbon before her eyes began to droop.

Which means I still don't have any fucking answers—though, at least she's fed and resting.

And in danger.

From my life?

Or hers?

I hate you.

I'm just...sorry.

As opposite as those sentences are, I know she meant both of them.

Without my shoulder to lean against, she starts to slump. I catch her and Jace helps me tuck a pillow under her head. I snag a blanket from the back of the couch, wrap it around her, then follow him down the hall and out the front door.

He crosses his arms. "You going to fix this?"

"I *thought* I fixed it before."

"You know what *I* thought of that decision," he mutters.

"Yeah." He made it pretty fucking clear I was making the worst mistake of my life.

And considering what remains of the woman I once loved, the woman who ate tonight like she hasn't had enough food for five years, then fell asleep like she's been hovering on the brink of exhaustion that entire time, I know, without a doubt, that he's not wrong.

"She really hit you hard enough to give you that?" A nod at my cut temple.

"Sort of. I slipped and hit my head on the desk after she kicked me in the junk hard enough to almost make me pass out."

His brows fly up. "That's not the Briar I know."

"I'm not sure the Briar we know exists any longer."

He sighs. "Fuck, man. This is a mess."

I don't say anything.

Because what the fuck *can* I say?

"You want me to look into the files she stole?"

"Nah. I already know what it was she took."

His brows fly up. "Corporate espionage?"

"No, they were personal."

"*How* personal?"

"About as fucking personal as it can get." My temple throbs and I reach up, barely catching myself before I rub at the still-healing cut there. "My dad's journal."

He curses.

"Yeah. He left it to me in the will and I read all of ten pages before I shut it in the safe."

"That was enough?"

"To remind me of the bastard he was?" I nod. "Abso-fucking-lutely. The real question is who knew it was there in the first place, and what their connection to Briar is."

"I'll look into it. Want me to loop in Jean-Michel?"

I hate the idea of anyone else knowing about my fucked-up family and the horrible things they were responsible for, but if anyone can find out things I won't be able to, it's Jean-Michel.

"If he's willing to help me on this, I'll owe him."

Jace's mouth quirks. "I know he'll take you up on that."

"I wouldn't expect anything else."

He pauses...then his smirk fades, his gaze boring into mine. "I also need to make it explicitly clear that you will *not* hurt her again."

I wave a hand at my temple, mutter flippantly, "I don't think that's a problem, man. Especially with air freshener in reach."

She'd brought the can to the coffee table, setting it on the glass surface.

A reminder.

But also within arm's reach.

Jace steps closer, still spearing me with his eyes. "Don't make a fucking joke. Not now. Not about her." He clamps his teeth together and looks away. "You didn't see her that day, after you left. You didn't have to get her off that mountain or set up her new life—"

My temper starts to burn. *I* was there. *I* said the words and watched her heart break.

I left. I had to.

For her own good.

For her safety.

For—

"And what happened to that?" I snap. "She was supposed to have an apartment, money. She was *supposed* to be safe and secure and—"

"Supposed to be means fucking nothing and you know it," he snaps back. "As far as I knew, she was using the money. It's not like I had access to the account to check its balance and you sure as fuck weren't sharing any details."

No. I'd closed myself off to everything.

Everyone.

Sighing, he shoves his hand through his hair. "The last time I checked in on her was about six months after you broke it off. I tracked her down at work and she asked me—no, she *begged* me to stay away from her, said every time I came by it was setting her back, that it was like she was on that mountain again, watching you walk away from her."

Fuck.

"That's when she told me she was selling the apartment and moving. When she asked me to give her the space to do that, to have a fresh start." He looks away, jaw clenching. "You didn't see her, man. Not in the aftermath. Not as she tried to pull the pieces of her life together." His gaze comes back to mine. "I had to let her go."

And now we're here.

I nod, chin dropping to my chest, my sigh forceful, regret sitting heavily in my chest. "Yeah, I know the feeling."

He's quiet for a long, long moment.

Then he murmurs, "I know you do." He squeezes my shoulder. "I call Pascal, Jean-Michel, and we'll figure this shit out, I promise. But right now, you need to get back inside. She needs...a doctor, a nutritionist, a fucking therapist. She needs to feel safe. And she needs to know the truth of why you left that day."

I promised myself she would never be dragged into the nightmare of my family's legacy.

I promised myself she would only have freedom and safety and as much care as I could provide.

I promised myself I would never hurt her.

And given the woman she is today, it's clear I broke every single one of those vows.

"I'll tell her." His brows lift. "And arrange for the rest."

A nod. "We'll help too."

"I know you will."

A nod. Then he turns for the elevator, but before he hits the button, he stops, glances back at me. "Brooks?"

"Yeah?"

His expression goes as hard as steel. "You hurt her again and you'll be nursing a fuck of a lot more than a bruise to the temple."

Inclining my head, I acknowledge the well-deserved warning.

Then I walk back into my apartment, lock the door, and head straight for the living room, for the couch.

Only...it's empty.

Briar's gone.

FOURTEEN

BRIAR

I CLOSE MY EYES, lifting my face into the breeze.

It's slightly too brisk, cold enough to raise goose bumps on my skin, but I don't go inside.

I *can't* go inside.

Not when the moonlight and the stars beckon, drawing me into the past.

Another night. Another couch. Another man.

Another *lifetime*.

And now I need to shut the door on it.

I'll tell him the truth, deal with the fallout, and then we can both move on, untangle this twisted-up knot that's drawn us back together—before he can turn himself into my savior and me into the damsel in distress again.

Before he destroys me again.

I turn around and gasp, not having heard him come out onto the balcony behind me. He's leaning back against the wall, arms and ankles crossed and, God, why does he have to be so fucking handsome?

Those deep brown eyes. The dark stubble on his cheeks. That chiseled jaw. Broad shoulders. Strong arms. Narrow waist. Thick thighs. An ass I can't see...

But that I got caught watching time and again during our brief relationship.

It's a really nice ass.

"I can't get the USB back," I say. "And I don't know what's on it, but I'm guessing it's not good because they wanted it."

He doesn't move, just keeps his ankles and arms crossed and stares at me.

"What charity did you donate the money to?"

I still, the ice I'd been trying to gather around me shattering and falling to the wayside. "Wh-what?"

"The charity you donated the money I left for you. Which one was it?"

I dig my toes into the soles of my boots, trying to figure out why he's asking.

Is he going to take it back?

"It was four years ago now," I say quietly. "I think they've probably already spent it."

"I know."

The silence stretches, broken only by the faint metallic *click* of a flagpole, the *whoosh* of traffic below, the occasional airplane soaring overhead.

"So what charity?" he finally asks.

I weigh whether to tell him for another long moment.

But what are the chances of him dropping this?

Not great.

And really, is it going to matter one way or another?

The man I knew wouldn't take money from a charity.

You don't know this man.

Maybe I never knew Brooks at all.

Sighing, I shake my head...and name it.

He doesn't react for what feels like an eternity. Then his mouth kicks up. "Horses, huh?"

I look away, my throat suddenly tight, my eyes burning.

Then I shrug. "They're innocent."

His eyes drop from mine and he nods then pushes off the wall. "Come on," he says, his voice unreadable and soft enough to barely reach my ears. "It's cold."

He walks inside.

By the time I pick my jaw up from the floor and follow him, he's at the fridge, snagging a beer. He lifts one in my direction and I shake my head.

My stomach is stuffed—full to the brim with omelets and pizza and the couple of bourbons I had earlier.

Yet when he grabs the milk out and starts making a mug of hot chocolate, my dessert stomach wakes up, rumbling softly.

"It's for you," he says as though he's somehow heard it even from all the way across the room. He puts the mug in the microwave, jabs at the buttons, then turns for a cabinet, tugging open the door.

The bag of marshmallows he pulls out makes my heart squeeze.

The microwave dings and he retrieves the mug, topping it with a truly absurd amount of marshmallows.

"Here," he murmurs, pressing it into my hand.

"I...thanks," I whisper.

He snags his beer and comes back over. "What happened?"

"With what?" I hedge, plucking out a marshmallow.

He just looks at me.

And God, I don't want to tell him.

I have to, though.

I have to end this shit.

"They came not long after I donated the money and moved

into my own apartment. I was working at a vet clinic answering the phones but figured I'd go to tech school so I could eventually help with the animals."

"You would be good at that."

"Yeah," I whisper.

"Then what happened?"

I fight back a shudder as I set my hot chocolate aside.

His eyes flick to it then back to mine.

"A woman approached me, said she had a great job opportunity. I didn't trust her, obviously, and turned her down. Then someone else made an approach, and he *really* didn't like it when I turned him down too. But I didn't relent—I had a job, a place to live. I didn't need a 'great' opportunity."

His chest rises and falls on a breath, like he knows the worst is coming.

And it is.

"At first, it seemed like nothing—notes in my mailbox I just threw away. But then I started finding them in my apartment."

He goes stiff.

"Not shoved under the door or anything, but"—this time I can't hold back the shudder and it vibrates through me so violently I'm glad I put the mug of hot cocoa down—"on my kitchen counter, my nightstand, next to my toothbrush." I pause. "In my underwear drawer."

His expression darkens.

"I just threw them all away, knew it couldn't be anything good." I sigh. "And then I lost my job."

He curses.

"I'd given the money away, so I didn't have much of a safety net, and even though I applied everywhere, I couldn't get a new position. So eventually...I was evicted." I nibble at the corner of my mouth. "But it wasn't until I was living out of my car that things got really bad."

He sets his beer beside the mug. "How bad?"

I don't want to think about that time. "What was on the flash drive?"

"My father's personal journal and enough information to ruin my family."

No hesitation in unleashing the bomb he just dropped.

"I...what?"

"How'd it get really bad?"

I blink once. Twice. "Ruin your family?"

"My father was a bastard—you knew that much."

I nod.

"Well, he liked to keep a record of precisely how much... and all the unsavory ways he was creating our family's legacy."

"Umm..."

"For the record, that includes blackmail, corporate espionage, and even on a few occasions, human trafficking."

My mouth has dropped open.

I can feel it.

But I can't make myself stop gaping at him.

"I don't give a fuck what the old bastard did and I don't give a fuck if it ruins my name, ruins *me*—I looked the other way plenty of times and know my own reckoning might come if that drive gets out. But I don't care about me. I care about *you*." He leans closer. "What happened when you were living out of your car?"

I'm blinking again.

Once. Twice.

"You care about me?"

"Yes. Now tell me, baby. What the fuck happened to you?"

FIFTEEN

BROOKS

HER MOUTH DROPS OPEN AGAIN, and it's so fucking cute when she does that.

So cute I want to lean in and taste her shock on my tongue.

But I have the feeling that'll just end up with me being blinded by air freshener.

And I need my eyes.

So I can keep staring at her.

Thin—too thin—but still the most beautiful woman I've ever seen. Pale blue eyes, that hair of moonlight, a body I want to fall to my knees and worship.

But more than the outside, it's always been the person Briar is on the inside that overshadows everything else.

So damned beautiful it takes my breath away.

Even if that beauty is tempered by anger.

Because right now she's fucking pissed.

"You care about me?" she asks again.

"Yes. Now—"

"You *care* about *me?*"

"Yes, baby, I—"

"Did you care about me when you said, *I don't?*" she snaps and I open my mouth, but I don't get the chance to reply before she goes on, "You know I heard those words over and over again for years? Every time I'd close my eyes, I'd see your face go cold, hear those fucking words a-and—"

Her voice breaks.

And part of my heart breaks.

And...the words just pour out of me.

"I got the first letter the night after I put a ring on your finger. You were in the bath, doing whatever it was you did in there." I try to smile, but I know it's a fucking facsimile by the way the anger fades from her face.

"What?"

"I went to grab something from my office. It was sitting dead center on my desk. At first I thought my assistant left it there for me. Found out pretty quickly that wasn't the case. That's when I started investigating."

"And adding security," she whispers.

I nod. "It didn't matter how many guards I added or monitoring systems we installed...they kept coming."

"What did they say?"

Rage crawls up my spine, through my shoulders, along my neck, into my jaw. "What did yours say?"

She shifts closer, eyes searching mine. "They threatened me?"

"My businesses at first, but they were too protected." My dad might have been a right bastard, but he'd made sure they were ironclad...except for the journal. That could have ruined all of his carefully made plans, if he was still alive—and if I hadn't done everything in my power to protect the businesses since his death.

Thousands of people rely on what he built, on their jobs at the company, on the research they conduct.

But I can't lie and say I've turned into a philanthropist who's going to donate every penny to charity and live off the land.

The money gives me power, strength, flexibility—

And I still walked away from the woman I loved.

And...put her through hell in the process.

My temple throbs.

But I push that aside, stifle the regret before it can eat me alive.

I can let that happen later, when I'm awake and staring at the ceiling, sleep too fucking far away.

"Then you. I doubled security and they sent me a close-up picture of you reading in the garden. Tripled it and it was a photo of us kissing in the kitchen." I'd been wiping away a dollop of whipped cream from her top lip, had been unable to resist leaning in and tasting it on my tongue. "Turned the place into a fucking fortress and I found a picture of you sleeping in bed tucked into my nightstand."

She gasps.

And for a second, I'm right back in that moment.

The fear—the complete and abject terror—feeling out of control, unable to fix it, even with so many resources at my disposal, and the slow, inexorable crawl of knowledge that to save her, I was going to have to give her up.

"And in the car..." I close my eyes, almost able to feel the paper of the envelope on my fingertips again.

"What?"

"There was a picture of you getting ready."

"For what?"

Slowly, I reach out and take her hand, needing the feel of her skin instead of the sensation of that fucking memory.

The small slice of pain as the paper cut into my thumb.

The horror of the image...and the beauty of the woman I loved.

Part of me expects her to pull back.

God knows I deserve it.

Except it's almost worse than that.

Because her hand remains limp in mine.

I hate you.

Fuck, what am I doing?

I start to draw away when—

Her fingers tighten on mine. "For the wedding ceremony?"

I nod.

"That's why you walked away?"

It's why I gave them what they wanted—a house in France, another in Germany, the rights to several patents.

And it's why I left Briar.

Because I knew that if I stayed, if there was any hint of connection, or me watching out for her, or contact, she would be right back at risk again.

I couldn't let that happen.

So I left it to Jace.

And he...I want to be pissed at him because he clearly didn't make sure she was good.

But I get why he left her alone, why she said she needed it.

So, while the anger is there, I know Jace's regret and guilt is burning almost as brightly as what I'm feeling.

Well, maybe not *almost*.

"Brooks," she says softly.

"Yes," I rasp. "It's why I left you."

Her fingers tighten almost painfully around mine.

Then she slips her hand free.

My heart twists.

But when she picks up the mug, takes a sip, something settles in me.

It's like for the first time in five years, I can finally breathe.

SIXTEEN

BRIAR

MY HEAD IS SPINNING, my heart breaking with what he's
shared.

Photos.

Letters.

Violations designed to scare, to break down, to separate
us.

And it worked.

And...

The sip of hot chocolate sits heavily in my stomach and my
head is spinning.

"Can we just..." I tilt my head in the direction of the couch.
"...sit down?"

"Yeah, baby." And just like always—or like *almost* always, I
amend, my mind on that rainy mountaintop, my dress soaked
through, my carefully styled hair hanging limply around my
face, clinging to my cheeks, the chill seeping into my bones—he
gives me what I want.

He walks across the open space, settles on one end of the couch.

Since he forgot it, I snag his beer, bring it with me.

"Thanks," he murmurs when I hand it to him.

I nod in reply, sit on the other side of the couch, and look at my hot chocolate.

Mostly because I have no idea what to say.

As though sensing that, he fills in the emptiness with exactly what I need.

Not the painful past. Not the vast distance gaping between us.

He gives me something...light.

"You remember Jace's wife, Marie?"

I nod. Jace had spoken a lot about his wife while we ate pizza (and carefully avoided everything to do with me being back in Brooks's life and the way it all went so badly before). It was beautiful—the way his face softened, the tone of his voice.

I didn't even need to listen to his actual words to know how much he loves her.

It's clear as day.

And it made me ache and rage and...be so damned happy he had her.

That they had each other.

"I remember," I murmur.

"Want to know how they first got together?"

I nod again and then he's telling me a story about work rivals and a stolen Lyft and apartments on the same floor, about Marie's place flooding and Jace winning her over with cookies.

"I love that for him," I say when he finishes.

His mouth kicks up. "You'll love her too," he says.

As though I'm going to meet her.

As though I'm going to slot myself back into his life.

There's no way.

I can't let that happen.

"Brooks," I begin.

He leans over and takes the mug from my hands, sets it on the table. I hadn't even realized I'd been drinking it.

That it's empty.

"Come on," he murmurs after setting it in the sink.

"I need to get home."

"It's the middle of the night," he says gently. "Why don't you stay in the guest room and go home tomorrow instead?"

It's tempting.

But I should go.

No. I *have* to.

Only...I'm so tired and if I go home they can get to me.

They can get to me here too.

They can get to me anywhere.

"Come on," he says quietly, lightly touching my arm.

And though it's definitely a mistake, I let him lead me down the hall and into the guest room.

"Make yourself comfortable," he murmurs, opening one of the doors in the room, showing me a bathroom. "You're safe here."

I'm not safe anywhere.

But before I can say that or change my mind, he's walking out the door, closing it behind him...and the last thing I hear before it clicks shut is,

"I'm just down the hall if you need anything."

My feet move on their own volition, carrying me across the deeply masculine space and into the bathroom.

I gasp softly.

It's beautiful—the huge steam shower and the double sinks, plush rugs on the marble floor. The walls are painted the pale blue of an early summer morning and the cabinets are white. The whole space is airy and light and...

"When my chores were done, sometimes I would climb to the top of the hay loft. There was a little window there, dusty and forgotten. One morning, I got the courage to go out on the roof, to wipe it clean, and it was worth it. I would lie there staring up through that window, pretending I was a cloud in the sky, floating away until I was free."

He'd touched my cheek as he listened, his focus on me and only me.

And the blue on the walls is the exact shade I described.

I exhale, eyes sliding closed.

Hidden memories. Quiet mornings. Slivers of peace.

A man I thought would love me forever.

My eyes peel open and I move to the tub, unable to stop myself from being drawn to the sunken porcelain bath, unable to not I look *up*.

And feel something deep in my chest hitch.

Because there's a skylight there.

A place to stockpile hidden peaceful moments with the freedom of the sky overhead.

"Dammit, Brooks."

I really need to go.

I start to turn away but then my gaze catches on a glass jar sitting in the corner of the tub and I freeze, that damn hitch in my chest making itself known again.

The jar is heavy but the plastic seal has been removed, so I screw off the lid.

Untouched, though the familiar scent of roses and vanilla surrounds me, taking me back to another lifetime, another house.

"I love the way you smell." He kissed my temple. *"No matter what you're wearing."* A nip to my ear that made me shiver. *"Most especially when you're wearing nothing at all and I'm kneeling between your legs, my mouth—"*

I clamped my hand to that dangerous, delicious mouth. "Behave."

A flick of his tongue to my palm before he peeled my hand free. "That's what you say now"—his eyes burn into mine—"but later tonight..."

I rolled my eyes, put the jar of body scrub back on the shelf, and started for the front of the store.

"Why aren't you getting it?" he asked, following me.

"Because it's stupid expensive," I said over my shoulder. "And I don't need it."

I wasn't lying back then—I *hadn't* needed it.

Brooks took care of me, spoiled me far too much and far too often.

Including that day.

Because when I went up that night to take a bath...

There was a jar on the edge of the tub.

And it was never empty.

It's been five years since I've smelled it.

Five years since I've taken a bath.

I couldn't make myself sink into the small tub in my apartment, the dingy ones at the motels I stayed in.

But tonight I can't stop myself from reaching for the tap.

And filling the bath with hot, *hot* water.

SEVENTEEN

BROOKS

I HEAR the water start running and breathe a sigh of relief.

She's changed so much...but at least one small thing is the same.

She can't resist the allure of a bath.

I slump, leaning back against the wall, dropping my chin to my chest.

"Fuck," I whisper.

But I only give myself a moment to let the guilt run free and slice at me.

Then I'm shifting, pushing off the wall, and going down the hall to my office. I need to figure out who the fuck is doing this to us—no, to *her*.

Because I haven't had a single note, a single threat, not in the five years since I gave them what they wanted.

Not since I left Briar.

Because they had *her* to do their dirty work.

I exhale as those lashes of pain slice through my middle again.

Then I lock it down and get to work, sitting at my desk and pulling out my phone. It's beyond late to be calling in favors, but I can't just do nothing.

I've done that for five years.

And what did that get me? Get Briar?

But it wasn't until I was living out of my car that things got really bad.

I still don't have the full story, but I know that bad—*really bad*—in Briar's book is—

"Fuck," I whisper again.

Really bad.

I close my eyes and try to think.

Try to plan.

But I'm not any better off today than I was five years ago.

How can I get rid of a threat that seems to have eyes everywhere, that can penetrate any line of defense?

The estate has guards and cameras and security layer upon security layer—

That Briar seemed to penetrate without a problem.

Despite the seriousness of the situation, my lips turn up at the corners.

She's always been tough, a survivor. But the core of her is sweet and kind, so fucking kind that when she smiled at me, when she touched me, cared for me...it was like I was the only one in the world the sun was shining on in that moment.

I vowed to protect that core.

Now I'm wondering if it's been dimmed forever.

"The extra security is already on its way."

"You need to make sure they blend in. I'm fairly certain they're surveilling the building."

"We're good at moving in the shadows," Pascal says.

"Considering how much you cost," I mutter. "I fucking hope so."

"This one's on the house."

My eyebrows fly up.

"I fucked up." His voice is even, but I can see the rage under the surface. "I should have kept eyes on her."

"We thought *I* was the one putting her at risk."

Removing myself from her life should have fixed everything.

Instead, it just made everything so much worse.

"Another mistake," he growls. "But I'm going to fix it." A breath as he tucks his anger away and gets down to business. "The security at the estate hasn't been upgraded since I was working for you full time"—before he left to start his own security company—"but clearly I'm not happy with the group we subcontracted to run it day-to-day. I'll get my team to coordinate the move to someone who's actually competent." He scowls. "There was an accident the morning that Briar broke in —a drunk woman crashed her car into the front gate—"

I frown.

I hadn't heard that.

"Rookie shit," he mutters, shaking his head. "The woman didn't even hit the gate hard enough to dent it, but she was certainly 'drunk and disorderly' enough to serve as a distraction to give Briar time to work." A sigh. "They should have known better and responded by following procedure."

We talk about how she got in, about the window and the safe, and make some notes to change codes and procedures and replace the window altogether—if Briar knew the security, someone else might too.

"I've learned a lot in the last five years," he says. "And now I have some guys on my team who excel at finding security holes and plugging them—"

"How's that?"

His mouth curves up in the barest hint of a smile. "They might have had a little practice exploiting them before coming to work for me."

Despite the circumstances, I chuckle.

"I'll get those guys on reviewing the system and strengthening it." He stands up. "In the meantime, we'll be in touch regularly, and I'll also send someone to Briar's apartment to see what we can find there."

That's a good idea. "I'll get the address from her when she wakes up and pass it along."

"No need," he says. "I have it already."

I blink.

Then feel a tiny bit of the weight that's been steadily settling on my shoulders over the last hours, the last *years* lift.

"Okay," I say. "Thanks."

"It's our job—or it should have been." His jaw flexes then he exhales. "Right. We'll get the preliminaries in place, start investigating, and report back to you once I know something. In the meantime, try to keep your normal routine as much as possible."

"I'm not sending her home."

He pauses, but only for a second, and when he speaks, there's a hint of steel in his words that both lifts the hairs on my nape and calms the twisting, painful maelstrom in my gut. "No, you're not. You're keeping her with you and we're going to make sure she's safe."

We exchange our goodbyes, and he leaves.

The silence that surrounds me is heavy, as is the darkness.

Pieces in place.

A plan to move forward.

And not one fucking thing resolved.

So much for the tornado of guilt and regret, yearning and rage being calmed.

Groaning, I rub my hands over my face and lean back in my chair—

The same moment a piercing scream echoes down the hall.

I'm up and moving before the sound cuts off, rounding my desk, pounding out of my office, lurching for the door to my bedroom—because I wouldn't put her anywhere else, because I had no intention of letting her sleep anywhere but my bed, my space, my *arms*.

And because the guest bath doesn't have a tub.

I shove through the door, race across the carpet to find...

My bed empty.

Heart pounding, mind racing, I spin, thinking that somehow someone got in, that someone got *her*...

That the nightmare is happening all over again.

Then I see her.

Curled up in the corner of the room between the dresser and the wall.

The rage ramps up as I move closer, as I see a pillow and blanket from the bed tucked behind and around her, respectively.

She whimpers and I tamp it down, crouching.

Her eyes are closed, her head thrashing from side to side, hair tangled, hands clenched on the edge of the blanket, knees tucking up tighter and tighter.

A nightmare.

The rage flares again, but I force myself to move carefully, slowly, to speak calmly, softly.

"Briar, baby," I murmur. "Wake up."

She whimpers again and I brush her hair back.

"It's just a dream," I soothe. "It's not real, and I'm here now. You can wake up."

Another whimper. "Br-Brooks." She thrashes, dislodging my hand. "No. Don't— *Please,* I need you."

I rock back as the impact of that hits, eyes sliding closed.

I hold myself still for a long, long moment, trying to contain all that I'm feeling, wishing with every cell in my body, I could turn back time.

That I could give it all up, make it so I never ruined her life.

So I never knew her.

Never brought my stain to her world, never caused her pain, never—

Soft fingers on my cheek startle me and my eyes fly open.

EIGHTEEN

BRIAR

I CAN STILL ALMOST FEEL the raindrops on my skin, dripping down my hair, my back, between my breasts, leaving me chilled and numb.

But right now it's another drop of liquid that has me frozen down to the bone.

I woke to a man crouched in front of me and my past has taught me that's dangerous, that I should run and hide, do my best to escape...

Because bad things are coming.

Except the only *bad thing* in this moment is the pain written into the lines of Brooks's face.

And the tear sliding down his cheek.

I'm reaching up before I realize I've moved, lightly rubbing the drop from his skin.

My touch has his eyes flying open, dislodging another tear.

I wipe that one away too.

Neither of us say anything as the moment stretches, only

silence between us. It grows heavy, emotions from our past clinging to the present, to the future.

Then he shifts, his weight altering ever so slightly—as though he's going to pull away, going to stand, going to leave me.

And it's like I'm back in the dream, back on the mountain, back watching him walk away from me.

I lurch forward, launching myself into his arms.

We tip backward, the plush carpet breaking our fall.

Though, really, it's Brooks who's cushioning me against the impact, his arms wrapping around me, his body beneath mine. His scent in my nose, his gentle words in my ears, his hand weaving into my hair, protecting the back of my skull from the threat of impact.

Protecting me from an invisible threat.

I freeze.

And the ice inside me ruptures, a wealth of emotions flowing out, flooding my senses and...

I burst into tears.

Five *years* of tears are torn out of me.

Brooks holds me closer and sits up, arms wrapping even tighter around me. "It's okay, baby. I'm here. I'm here," he repeats. "I'm here."

Here now.

But for how long?

Here now.

But when will he break me again?

Here now.

But how can I possibly forgive him?

I distantly hear a strange sound, something that almost sounds like an animal, and it takes me a minute to realize it's me. That I'm making the noise, and I try to stop, try to find the strength to pull away.

Only, I can't.

Especially when he gets to his feet and carries me across the room, climbing into the bed that smelled of him, a bed I couldn't bear to sleep in.

Not without him.

So I'd contented myself with a pillow that was rich with his scent, a pillow I pretended was his warm body.

Even though it made me weak.

Even though I should have marched down the hall and demanded he let me sleep in the *real* guest room.

Or better yet, I should have quietly walked down the hall and exited his life, leaving him far, far behind.

So he couldn't hurt me again.

So I didn't hurt him again either.

Now as he climbs into bed, curling me against his chest, still murmuring those soft, reassuring words, I can't make myself pull away, can't imagine walking out, can't so much as form the image in my head.

I just...cry.

And let him hold me the entire time.

I DON'T REMEMBER FALLING asleep, but the moment my eyes peel open, sunshine pouring in through the windows, I know that Brooks is awake.

And that he hasn't slept a wink.

I feel it in the tension in his body, in the strain of his emotions licking at the air.

When I put a hand to the mattress and push up, his arms fall away and I'm able to see his face, and yup—definitely didn't sleep a wink.

His hair is mussed, the stubble on his cheeks thick, but his eyes are alert, the dark circles beneath them so black they almost look bruised.

"You okay?" he asks quietly.

I nod.

He slowly lifts a hand but pauses before he touches me.

I lean in, close the distance between my cheek and his palm. "Liar," he murmurs, lightly stroking his thumb over my skin, the slight rasp making me shiver.

He tugs the blankets more tightly around me.

Then explains why he called me a liar.

"You're exhausted and your body's aching."

He's not wrong.

I feel like I got run over by a Mack truck, my throat sore and my shoulders and back muscles throbbing from all the crying.

Before I can admit that, he's slipping out of bed.

I watch him until he disappears from sight, not understanding…

Until I hear the water turn on, filling the tub.

And my heart squeezes.

He comes out, our gazes sliding by each other's as he moves out of the bedroom, footsteps soft on the hardwood floor in the hall.

I wait, but when he's gone for more than a couple of minutes I decide I'd better check on the water in the tub so I climb out of bed and do just that.

It's nearly full so I take care of the necessary bathroom needs.

When I'm washing my hands, Brooks walks back in, a cup in his hand and a bag in the other. "Toothbrush," he says quietly as he puts the plastic bag beside me on the counter. "Tea," he adds when he sets down the mug.

It's steaming, tangling with the damp air and filling the room with the soft hints of chai.

"You hungry?"

I shake my head.

After all the food from last night, I'm still full.

"Sure?"

"Yeah," I rasp.

His eyes flick to my throat and then the mug is being pressed into my hand. "Drink," he orders. "It'll help."

I take a sip and he's not wrong, the pleasant warmth helps soothe the ache there.

"Are you okay?" I ask softly.

Then sip again when his eyes flare with emotion.

He's exhausted and guilty and worried.

I put the mug down and walk into his arms.

He doesn't move, stays stiff as a statue until I murmur, "It's okay."

Then he shudders, his head dropping, his arms banding around me, holding me so freaking tightly I can barely breathe.

But that's okay.

Because he needs this.

Same as I needed to shed all those tears last night.

I don't know what's going to happen to us, how the wounds we both carry could ever be healed.

I just know I need to hold him.

That we need to hold each other.

NINETEEN

BROOKS

"SO I'M JUST SUPPOSED to sit around and do *nothing?*"

Pascal leans back against the doorframe, eyes scanning the room in a way that tells me he's seen and assessed everything but he's still not letting his guard down.

Like a threat may come from any angle.

I appreciate that, I really do.

But seriously, what the fuck am I supposed to do?

"Listen to the man with security experience?"

I sigh.

"I'm not saying sit in your tower and wait around for us to rescue you both—"

"You're not?"

He's just given me strict orders on the places I can go (this apartment, my office building, Jean-Michel and Jace's houses), on the people I can speak to (work is fine under all normal capacities, the situation with Briar, no one, with the exception of Jace and Jean-Michel because they've been "briefed" too), even on the way I have to act outside the house.

Be myself.

Luckily, I'm mostly a bastard so that front won't be hard to maintain.

Pascal rolls his eyes. "I get that what I'm asking isn't easy, but we found monitoring at Briar's apartment and on her car. We need to buy some time to investigate that. I also need to speak with her, see what she knows about these people. Having a source on the inside will be invaluable."

"No."

His eyebrows fly up.

"She's been through enough," I mutter. "There's no way I'm making her relive it all over again. Find another way."

"It'd be easier if she—"

"*No*," I growl. "I don't give a fuck if it's easier. She's staying out of this, and your only job is to make sure she's safe."

Something settles over his face, but I can't read it.

Maybe respect. Maybe frustration. Maybe solidarity.

Or a mix of all three.

Whatever he's feeling, he doesn't get a chance to reply because his head suddenly whips toward the hall, his entire body on alert. I feel a chill skate down my spine, but even as I'm processing that, I'm watching his body relax as he dismisses the threat.

Briar walks into view. "Pascal?"

He inclines his head but doesn't otherwise move.

"It's, um, good to see you again. It's been a long time."

"Yes."

She's wearing the same pants and shirt as last night and I scowl.

But she's not looking at me.

All her focus is on Pascal—who's staring at her, assessing her...but still hasn't moved.

"Are you here to bring me in?" she asks suspiciously, hand settling on her thigh.

On the bulge there.

My scowl fades.

Pascal keeps his arms and ankles crossed, and I know he's spotted the lump in her pocket too.

The can of air freshener.

And he likes the idea of her thinking of it as a weapon about as much as I do.

That's to say, not at all.

"No," he says tersely.

Her eyes come to mine and I nod, explaining, "He's going to figure out what's going on and help us track down the people responsible for it."

She exhales, hand dropping to her side. "I should talk to you, tell you what I know. I'll help you get Brooks out of this."

I open my mouth to protest.

But then she says something worse.

"Then I'm leaving."

Pascal blinks—and that's about as surprised as his face gets.

"We don't need to talk about that right now," I say. "You should be resting." I can't help my eyes from trailing over her too-thin body. "And eating."

Her cheeks go pink and she glares at me before turning to Pascal. "What do you want to know?"

A pause that speaks volumes before he replies dryly, "What *you* know."

"Did Brooks tell you what I told him?"

A nod.

"Then I guess you know what I know." She spins on her heel, disappears into the hall.

"Where are you going?" I call.

Her head pops back into view. "Home."

Then she's gone again.

Pascal's eyebrows lift as he glances in my direction.

"I know," I mutter, and I'm already moving, brushing by him and intercepting Briar just as she reaches the front door.

Christ, this is getting old.

I snag her shoulder—

And promptly find myself pinned face first against the wooden panel, my arm pulled back with enough force that pain is rippling along the front of my shoulder, that I know one wrong move will leave me with a dislocated joint.

"Don't touch me," she grits out.

"Briar," I say, reaching back with my other hand and grabbing her wrist. Not tightly, but firmly enough to ground her in the here and now. "It's me."

She hisses out a breath but doesn't release me.

Not for a long moment.

Then her hands open and my arm is free.

I slowly turn to face her, but I don't move away from the door. This new Briar can kick my ass, but threat of dislocation or not, I'm not just going to let her walk out.

I *can't*.

"You can't grab me like that," she whispers, gaze on her feet.

"I'm sorry."

She looks up, eyes going wide. "You're sorry?"

"I didn't mean to scare you," I say, uncertain of her tone. I can't read it. She's not mad, exactly. It's more like she's...astonished? "It's not safe for you to leave," I explain.

"You're sorry?" she asks again.

"Yeah, baby. I—" I shake my head. "This is a mess and it's complicated and it's *dangerous*. I can't let you leave."

She opens her mouth.

"But more than the danger, than not knowing what's happening and who these fuckers are that hurt you...it's that I *can't let you leave.*"

"You had no problem doing that five years ago."

"I had a problem, baby," I rasp. "It fucking tore me apart to walk away that day."

Raindrops in her hair. Joy in her laughter.

Then...the wounded look on her face.

The empty house.

My empty *life.*

"I had to. You know why. You lived it. And it kills me that it doesn't matter." I touch her cheek. "That despite me leaving, despite me giving them what they asked for, you still went through what you went through. I wish I'd done something different, *anything* different. I wish I hadn't walked away, wish I could go back and change it."

"Brooks," she says quietly, her tone—

Fuck, I can't take that cool disappointment in her tone.

"But I can't, baby. I know I can't make it right. I know I can't do enough for you to forgive me, I get that. I'm not asking for your forgiveness. I'm just asking"—my eyes burn again and I clear my throat, push on—"no, I'm *begging* for you to let me find a way to get you safe. For real this time. Then if you want to go, I'll let you go. I promise."

Those light blue eyes are unreadable as they hold mine for long, long moments.

"Okay," she eventually murmurs.

Relief ripples through me and I open my mouth to reply—

Right as there's a knock on the wooden panel behind me.

TWENTY

BRIAR

"STEP BACK, PLEASE," I hear even as I'm registering the knock.

Fear coils.

"What if—?"

Pascal glances at Brooks, who steps forward, wraps his arm around my shoulders, and draws me back.

"What if it's them?" I whisper.

"It's not."

I frown. "How do you—?"

"Because my team would have called," Pascal says, his gaze holding mine and there's something about the cool confidence, the utter assurance in the statement that has my pulse slowing down, calm surrounding me. "But it never hurts to be careful, right?"

I nod.

That makes sense.

His eyes go to Brooks again, and a moment later, I find

myself tucked around the corner, a big, masculine body between me and the front door.

I hear the lock disengage with a click, feel the slight rush of air as the door opens, and—

"Pascal."

The female voice is familiar, but I can't place it. Still, I can't miss that Brooks immediately relaxes and steps forward, leaving me alone as a group—yes, a *group*—of people walk into the living room.

A tall, broad older man with salt and pepper in his beard and hair, a curvy brunette trailing behind him, a shy smile on her face. Behind them are Jace and the woman who must be his wife, Marie. She's dressed in wide, flowing pants and a button-down, but it's her deep green eyes that capture my focus.

They're absolutely breathtaking.

So much so, it takes me a second to realize there's a third couple. My heart convulses when I see the tall, slender woman. She's holding an infant in her arms and a man is hovering beside her.

He's gorgeous, but he has a sort of lean, athletic grace that separates him from the other men in the room.

I can't put my finger on why, exactly—they're all in good shape, all can clearly handle themselves.

But there's something about the man with curly hair and the way he fills out a pair of jeans that makes it clear he's not a businessman...or someone with military experience, like Pascal.

The baby makes a tiny squawk and all the men freeze.

A moment later, the man with curly hair has scooped up the baby and is rocking it, the first man, Jace, and Pascal all shifting closer, as though ready to jump in and take over at the first inclination that something's gone wrong.

The only male who seems marginally less concerned is Brooks, though his attention goes to the baby all the same.

Why do I know—*know*—the little one already has every single one of these men wrapped around his or her little finger?

"Hi," I hear and tear my gaze away from Brooks in proximity to the baby.

And the yearning it creates.

And the pain.

"Hi," I say, shoving that down and shaking the proffered hand of the woman in the business attire.

"I'm Marie," she says.

"Oh," I exclaim. "Jace's wife. It's so nice to meet you. He talked about you a lot."

"Hopefully about all the good things and none of the annoying ones I do."

I open my mouth—

"You could never annoy me," Jace says, kissing the top of her head and slinging an arm around her shoulders.

"Hmm," she replies, clearly teasing as she taps a finger to her bottom lip. "I seem to remember a certain level of *annoyance* when I wanted to watch *Date My Ex* instead of playoff hockey."

"And *I* seem to recall you finding a way to make me less annoyed."

Pink on her cheeks. "Behave."

"Never."

"I'm Tiff," I hear from my side as I'm trying to survive the impact of Jace so in love with his wife and the mix of emotions I feel.

I'm so damned happy for him.

And I'm jealous.

"Briar," I say, shaking her hand.

"You know Jace and now Marie," she murmurs. "The big guy holding the baby is Rome and his wife is Chrissy—"

She nods at the other brunette, though I already knew who

she is from that night at the winery. My heart thunders, trying to pound its way out of my chest, leaving me a little breathless and lightheaded.

When Chrissy puts the pieces together...

"—and the scowly monster debating on snatching the baby from Rome is my husband, Jean-Michel."

The sound of his name has his head tipping up, full scowl in place. "I'm neither *scowly* nor a monster."

"Your expression says otherwise," she teases.

And I watch his face soften too.

Know it won't last long after he finds out what I was going to do to his daughter.

"Hi," Chrissy says, leaving the gaggle of men and introducing herself. "It's so nice to meet you. Sorry to intrude on your morning. We were having breakfast and Dad"—she tilts her head at Jean-Michel—"heard about what was happening and wanted to come over. Jace offered to bring him...and well" —she shrugs—"the rest of us are just nosy."

"But we brought treats!" Tiff says, holding up a robin's egg blue box.

"And alcohol," Marie adds dryly, showing me a bag with a couple of bottles of prosecco.

"And we'll go if you want," Chrissy chimes in, lifting a hand when Marie starts to protest. "Because we understand we're a big, noisy group that can be overwhelming—"

"But we hope you'll let us stay," Marie interrupts. "Because we're annoying, but we're also cool." She does finger guns in my direction. "I promise."

I blink. Once. Twice.

And still can't find the appropriate reply.

Chrissy snorts. "I told you not to do the finger guns." Then she grins. "Why don't we sit down and eat and drink something. Rome has a game tonight—"

THE BACHELOR AND THE BREAK-IN   121

"Go, Gold," Tiff says and my gaze ping-pongs to her smiling face.

"Rude," Chrissy grumbles, but it's also paired with a smile and an explanation. "My hubby plays for the Eagles and my dad owns the team." She waves a hand. "It was a whole thing, but we're good now."

I blink again.

"And Tiff used to nanny for one of the players on the Gold, who they're playing tonight."

"Oh," I manage to say.

Chrissy winces. "See? Overwhelming." She holds up the box again. "But good pastries make everything better, I promise."

"Right." I squeeze out, my throat feeling tight. "Of course. I, uh, just need to use the restroom." I start edging toward the hall. "Um, don't wait on my account to get started on the pastries. I'll be right back."

"We—" Marie begins.

But I'm already hurrying away.

And by the time my vision narrows to a tiny speck of light, black crawling in from its edges, I'm safely tucked in the corner of the bedroom, clutching the pillow that smells of Brooks, the blanket firmly pulled over my head.

TWENTY-ONE

BROOKS

I WATCH Briar hurry down the hall and spare only a second for the confused expressions on the women's faces before I follow her.

She rushes into my bedroom, closing the door behind her.

It clicks shut in my face and I spare another moment, this time longer, not wanting to invade her privacy, but also remembering another time, another life.

Too much.

Too fast.

She's not used to it.

She's spent far too much time isolated and alone and the last five years have only exacerbated that.

So, I turn the knob, open the door, and step inside, shutting it behind me.

My gaze searches the room, but it's like I already know where she's going to be.

Because my body is turning toward the corner—

And there she is, curled up beneath the blanket.

"Baby," I murmur, moving over to stand next to her.

I don't touch her this time, even though my greeting makes her go stiff. And quiet—for a long, long time.

"I'm fine," she says from beneath the blanket. "Go back to your friends. I'll be out in a minute."

Despite the worry gnawing at my bones, speaking to her like this—her voice slightly muffled by the blanket—makes my lips twitch.

"I know you're fine."

But I don't move, just settle on the carpet and lean back against the wall.

She goes quiet again.

I wait.

"If you know I'm fine, then why are you still here?"

"Ouch," I say lightly, though my amusement just continues to grow.

More still. More quiet.

The blanket lowers enough for me to see those gorgeous blue eyes, the strands of her moonlight hair scattered over her face. "I didn't mean—"

"I know." I slowly reach forward, brush away a lock that's clinging to her lashes. "Remember that charity event at the house?"

She freezes.

Then her mouth curves and it's fucking beautiful, that smile. "We really shouldn't have skipped out on the party."

"But we had fun."

"Yeah," she whispers, eyes drifting from mine and I know her brain is conjuring up the same memories as I am—stealing a bottle of champagne and a couple of trays of hors d'oeuvres and sneaking up into our room.

That had been the first time I'd joined her in that big soaking tub.

But it certainly hadn't been the last.

And by the time the party had broken up, I'd made sure every part of her body was thoroughly clean.

And she'd done the same for me.

"I thought someone would have missed us."

"Nah, they were all wrapped up in their own conversations." I wink. "Plus, Dolores was discreet—she probably shuffled everyone out the door the moment you started screaming my name."

"I did not!"

"Only because I muffled your moans with my hand."

She glares at me then shakes her head, her smile just beginning to tip up the edges of her mouth. "Maybe you're right." A beat. "Does Dolores still work for you?"

I shake my head. "She retired a few months back, but recommended her niece, River, to take over. She's great." I waggle my brows. "And she knows all of her aunt's secret recipes."

"Win-win."

I nod.

Her sigh is soft, thoughts returning to the past. "That was a good night."

"One of the best."

The silence stretches and I watch her face change, her eyes clouding with the same knowledge I'm feeling—that it was one of the best...and one of the last. "Don't," I rasp.

She doesn't pretend to not know what I mean. "We can't go back to the people we were then."

"I know."

"And you don't know me, not really, not anymore. Same as I don't know the person you are now. We've changed and too much time has passed and...we can't go back, can't pretend it didn't happen." Her voice drops to almost a whisper. "As much as we both wish that things might have been different."

"We don't need to go back." I pick up another strand of hair, lightly rubbing it between thumb and forefinger. Still so damned soft. "We just need to move forward."

"I don't think that's possible."

"Do you know that I kept the beanie you left behind the other night?"

Her brows drag together and she tilts her head to the side.

I get up, move to the nightstand, and open the drawer, pulling out the knit cap.

"Brooks," she whispers.

I bring it back over. "I saw your hair and part of me knew. But I couldn't accept it was you. Then I woke up with the hat in my hand, smelled you on the fabric, and I hoped. Now you're here. Now we have this chance." My heart starts thudding against my ribcage so damned hard I can barely breathe.

Something that becomes even harder to do when she shakes her head. "Too much time has passed. I...I want you to be safe, to not have these people messing with your life and I'll do what I can to make sure that happens."

"And you?" I ask, the question almost garbled from the rage that's threatening to boil over. "What about you?"

"You said it yourself. I'm a survivor." She shrugs. "I'll be good. Speaking of which"—she pushes the blanket back and starts to sit up—"we should get back out there."

"You're just giving up?" I ask, not retreating.

Especially when her movements mean that she's suddenly left mere inches between our bodies. "I'm not giving up. I'll stay until this is over, won't do anything to upset Pascal's investigation, especially when it might mean I can be free of..." She wavers here, throat working before she exhales and lifts her chin. "Especially if it means I can be free of it all, can make my own choices, live my own life for the first time."

The *without you* part is unspoken.

But I still hear it loud and clear.

"And what if you could have that and still have me," I murmur. "Still have *us*?"

She exhales, shakes her head. "Brooks," she says and her voice is gentle—gentle enough to wound. "That time is over for us."

"Is it?" I ask.

Her throat works again, and she nods.

But I see enough.

I see the heat in her eyes, the need, the hole inside her that only I can fill.

And yeah, that sounds dirty. But no, I don't mean it that way.

Not right in this moment, anyway.

"It is," she says. "There's nothing between us aside from memories and a current safety crisis. Once that's solved, you'll move on and I'll..."

"You'll what?" I ask, tucking a strand of her hair behind her ear.

She stills, throat working again and I can't miss that her pulse is fluttering at the base of her throat, so fast it's like her skin is vibrating. "I'll figure out what my next steps will be."

"And if I say those next steps will involve me?" I drag my fingers over her jaw, down the column of her throat, lightly brushing her skittering pulse.

"I'd say you're wrong."

"You think so?" *Thud-thud. Thud-thud. Thud-thud.*

Her chin lifts. "I *know* so."

"Hmm." I draw my finger along one collarbone. Then the other.

"Wh-what?" she asks.

"I think we should test that theory."

Her eyes go wide. "T-test?"

"Yeah, baby. *Test.*"

"How are you—?" I lean in and she sucks in a breath, cutting off the rest of her question.

That's okay, though.

I think we've spent more than enough time talking.

For the moment.

Which is why I lean closer and slowly, giving her plenty of time to stop me...

I brush my lips over hers.

TWENTY-TWO

BRIAR

I SHOULD HAVE TOLD him no.

Should have pushed him back, turned away.

He would have stopped.

I know he would have.

But some sick part of me, some pathetic and weak part wanted to be right here—his mouth on mine, his hands on my skin, his body pressed close.

So, I don't stop him.

I don't push him away.

And when his lips touch mine...I give in.

My mouth opens, my moan is soft as it glides from my tongue to his, and—

He groans, tightens his hold, the kiss intensifying. But it's not deep, not a tangle of lips and tongues, our hands moving to remove clothes and stoke desire. It's...*sweet*.

So beyond sweet my eyes prickle with tears and my heart rolls over in my chest, and I can't help but be sweet back. I trail my hands along his back and bring them forward, resting them on his pecs, feeling the strength of him, the warmth of him, the way his pulse pounds as rapidly as mine.

There's need in the rigid control of his body, but he doesn't release it.

Instead, he keeps the kiss gentle, reminding me of all the soft times, the easy times—stolen embraces in the garden, raindrops pattering on our heads when we got carried away and didn't see the weather change. Brushes of lips when he woke me in the morning, when we passed each other in the hall, when I came into his office to see him in the middle of the day, or when we stole down to the kitchen for a midnight snack.

So many memories.

So much good.

That's why it *hurt*.

And I don't want to hurt, not right now.

I don't want to think, don't want to miss and need and *ache*.

I just...*want*.

So freaking much.

And...hell, it's like just thinking that has everything I've been feeling exploding out from behind that shield I erected, the barrier that's continued to erode with each and every minute I've spent in his presence.

My nails dig into his chest and I press closer, loving the way his arms band tighter, his groan rumbles from his throat and into mine.

The kiss...oh God, this kiss isn't sweet.

It's deep and it's wet and—

"Oh!" I gasp as he rises to his feet, spinning and moving to the bed. He drops me on the mattress and comes over the top of me.

"Fuck." His lips trail along my jaw. "You are so damned beautiful."

I shiver, but that ice inside me has broken open and I'm feeling...so damned much.

The soft silk of his hair, the strength of his body, the heat of his skin, the slightly roughened tips of his fingers as he dips them under the hem of my shirt and trails them along my side.

"I'm different." My head drops back to the mattress, a moan tumbling from my lips as he kisses a sensitive part of my throat.

"But you're still you."

I shudder as the words vibrate through me, as they heal some wound deep inside me.

Then his fingers slide lower, slipping beneath the waistband of my pants, skating over my skin. Sensation explodes through me and instinct takes over.

Pleasure.

This man has given me pleasure, so much pleasure my body takes over, knows exactly what to do.

I part my legs, give him room to work.

And, God, he *works*.

Lightly drifting his fingers down, cupping me over my underwear and that big, hot hand has a moan tumbling from my lips, my hips arching, pressing more firmly against his palm. My need gathers, growing slick and damp, and his wolfish smile tells me what he's thinking, even before he says it.

"See? You're still you."

And, as he pushes my underwear aside, his fingers immediately finding that sensitive spot that never fails to make me moan, I'm inclined to agree with him.

To think that he might still be him too.

"Oh, God," I moan as he traces the folds of my labia, as he circles my clit, as he slides one thick finger inside, stroking it in and out, in and out, exactly as I like.

In the precise way that makes me crazy.

"I—"

He bends and slants his mouth over mine, kissing me long and deep, leaving me with lungs working in overdrive and a pulse thundering through my veins.

"Relax, baby," he murmurs. "Relax and let me make you feel good."

Impossible.

It's impossible to relax—mostly because he's playing my body like it's his instrument.

And maybe it is.

Because I can feel the pleasure swirling around my body, can feel it rolling through my cells, my nerves.

More. More. *More.*

Implosion.

"Brooks!" I cry, arching against his hand, fingers clawing at his shoulders.

Pleasure burns through me, leaving me limp and satiated and...in another lifetime.

He kisses me slowly and gently, coaxes me down, holding me close until my heartbeat settles and I manage to open my eyes.

"The time has passed?" he asks, humor in his tone even though his eyes are hot enough to scald.

I can barely lift my head, let alone process the words. "What are you talking about?"

"Nothing," he says, helping me sit up.

"Brooks," I begin again. "What—"

He straightens my clothes, brushes my hair back from my face. "Nothing."

"I—"

"Come on." He takes my hand, hauling me up from the bed.

"Brooks!"

"You need to eat."

Eat?

When he just gave me an orgasm that melted my bones and turned my head to mush?

When he's...

My eyes flick down.

When he's...*that*.

Hard, the fabric of his slacks cupping the rigid length of his erection, making me feel jealous.

I want to be the one doing the cupping.

He groans softly and my eyes shoot back to his, the sexy smile he's wearing stroking me between my legs. "Don't look at me like that, baby."

I want to do so much more than just cupping. "Why?"

Another groan. But this time, he snags my hand. "Come on, Trouble."

And as the impact of that—of another time, another life...or maybe, *maybe* it could be *this* life—he drags me out into the hall.

TWENTY-THREE

BROOKS

SHE HAS a pastry in her hand and another big mug of hot chocolate.

And she's smiling at something Chrissy's friend, Rory, is saying.

Rory showed up about ten minutes after we came out of the bedroom to knowing looks and smug smiles.

Thank God I paid all that money for soundproofing.

They still knew what we were doing down the hall.

They just couldn't hear it.

Worth it, even if they could.

I can still feel the slick evidence of her desire on my fingers, the clench of her muscles, can still taste her on my tongue and hear her moans and—

"She's not going to disappear, man."

I blink and turn toward Jace, mind shifting from the bedroom to the threat against her. "You sure about that?"

He winces. "Right. That was a shitty joke."

"Not on you," I say quietly.

"We'll figure it out," Jean-Michel says as he leans back against the counter, and I'd bristle at the way his eyes are locked onto Briar...if it wasn't the same exact way he looks at Chrissy.

And Marie.

And Rory, who showed up with her hockey-playing husband, his arms laden with bags.

All of which turned out to be filled with clothes and toiletries and shoes.

"Thanks for arranging for the clothes."

Briar's still wearing the uniform from the fundraiser, and even though I'd love to take her on a *Pretty Woman*-esque shopping spree, that wouldn't be smart.

Not until we know more.

Not until the threat against her is gone.

So though part of me fucking hates that someone else took care of her before I could, the rest of me is glad.

"I'll reimburse you."

He shakes his head. "I wouldn't accept it, for one. For another, it was Chrissy and the others. I had no part of it."

"A donation to her charity then."

Those blue eyes come to mine. "I heard you gave a big one at the event." Amusement begins to trickle into his expression. "Though we do have a litter of kittens that need—"

"No." I put my hands up. "Absolutely not."

That mischief grows as he calls, "Buttercup?"

My brows fly up at the non sequitur. Then further when Tiff turns toward him with a shy smile. "Yeah, honey?"

Buttercup.

Huh.

"Brooks has good news."

Her eyebrows drag together in confusion.

As do mine.

Mostly because I'm still stuck on the billionaire shouting endearments across the room as easily as he discusses security measures and business deals.

"What's that?" she asks, gaze flicking to mine.

"He and Briar are going to be foster parents."

Briar jerks, hot chocolate sloshing over the rim of the mug in her hand. She hurriedly sets it down, starts mopping up the mess, but her eyes are on mine.

And they are clearly saying, *What the actual fuck?*

And all I can silently communicate back is, *I have no fucking idea what this man is talking about.*

Which is fine—because we don't have long to wait for an explanation.

Rory squeals and hops to her feet. "Dogs or cats?"

"Cats," Chrissy says. "We just got a new litter in this morning."

Rory narrows her eyes at her best friend. "My foster system is nearly full."

"And mine is overflowing." Chrissy plunks her hands on her hips. "It's kitten season."

Marie leans back in her chair and sighs, not getting involved, just watching the standoff.

Likely this is far from the first (and the last) she's seen.

Tiff, meanwhile, is eyeing the friends with concern, and a glimpse of her nanny skills come out as she tries to negotiate a solution. "Maybe this isn't the best time for Brooks and Briar to take on—"

"Cats would be preferred."

All eyes go to Pascal, where he seems to have emerged from thin air to stand by the couch.

Last thing I knew, he was checking the sensors near the windows.

The man moves like a shadow.

Thank fuck he's on our side.

The women look at him and he shrugs. "Dogs need walks and to use the bathroom. The cats and Briar can hang out in here, where she'll be safe."

A blip of silence.

"Or maybe they don't need the stress of taking care of animals when they've already got a lot on their plates?" Marie points out.

"Fine," Rory grumbles, completely ignoring Marie as she looks over at Chrissy. "You win."

Chrissy grins.

"But *I* get first dibs during puppy season."

"Deal."

They shake hands and I drag my bewildered gaze from the deal that's just taken place over to Jean-Michel. "What just happened?"

Jace is the one who answers. "You just signed up to be a zoo, my friend."

"Say again?"

"It's better just to accept your fate now." Rome claps my shoulder, King nodding in agreement behind him.

"Remember how we were"—he does finger quotes—"just watching a dog for a few days?"

That dog now has a bed with its name embroidered on the front in several rooms of Jace's house.

"You told me that you decided to keep Gus."

"We did"—he winks at Marie when she glances over her shoulder and smiles at him—"but want to guess who brought us Gus to"—finger quotes again—"watch?"

I groan. "I seriously think this is the worst time to be taking on an animal—or *animals.*"

"Cats don't need much." He lightly punches my shoulder.

"And it might be good for her to have something to do that isn't..."

Thinking about the danger.

About the last five years.

About me walking away.

"Yeah," I mutter. "But if something happens to the cats..."

To *her*...

Jean-Michel shakes his head. "We suspect we know who's involved, and what we know is that the Lyons aren't particularly violent," he says. "Pain in the asses, yeah, and they're not above a kidnap and ransom, certainly. But they mostly hit us through our businesses, and they've never messed with the charities"—something pings in my mind at that statement, but he keeps talking and it slips from my thoughts just as quickly—"instead they'll hit you in other ways."

My temple throbs in protest to his words.

But I know that wasn't Briar's mission.

I know she wasn't trying to hurt me, not really. It was rage and anger and fear all coming together...and exploding.

Still, "Say that again when my woman isn't flinching when I go to touch her."

His eyes turn to ice. "What happened?"

"I don't know it all yet," I admit. "It's going to take time for her to trust me enough to open up."

"Seems like she trusted you plenty a few minutes ago," Jace says dryly.

"Don't make me punch you, asshole."

"I'd like to see you try."

King glances at Rome. "I thought us hockey players were supposed to be the violent ones."

He's looking down at his phone. "I'm too busy making a list of supplies Brooks needs for his house to talk shit."

I groan.

King jerks his chin toward the balcony. "We're definitely putting the cat tower there, right?"

I groan again, but even as I do that, I see Chrissy pointing her phone in Briar's direction. Her face melts at whatever is on the screen (though I guess I know *exactly* what Chrissy is showing her).

Which means I'm sunk.

My apartment is about to turn into a menagerie.

But I find I don't really care.

Because if it means she keeps smiling like that, I'll fill this fucking place with kittens.

Because if Briar stays long enough for me to make her safe, to let me love her again...

I'd give her the world.

TWENTY-FOUR

BRIAR

SO...CATS.

Or kittens, really.

I can't quite understand the sharp turn my life has taken over the last twenty-four hours, but if there's anything I've learned in my life, it's to adapt, press forward, and worry about the consequences later.

And take advantage of kittens when the opportunity presents.

"They're adorable," I murmur, passing Chrissy's phone back. "I'll figure out a way to get some supplies—"

Chrissy waves a hand. "Oh, not a chance."

"I—"

"We—the charity—provide everything. It's a big ask already to foster a rambunctious litter of fluffballs."

"But—"

"Litter box and litter, food and bowls, toys, brushes, carriers —they all go home with people who adopt. And for our foster moms and dads we add scratching posts and towers, water dispensers, plus everything else in multiples."

She smiles and it's nice and sweet and I try to tamp down the guilt I'm feeling.

Something that doesn't work.

Because she and her friends came by with food and have been really kind, even after I panicked and ended up doing things in the bedroom with Brooks that really shouldn't happen with company present.

And still, when I came out, my hair no doubt mussed and the evidence of what we did (something I'm *not* thinking about) written into the blush on my cheeks, they didn't comment.

Instead, I found out Chrissy had called her friend, Rory, and asked her to bring me clothes and shoes.

And makeup and shampoo.

And a hairbrush and a robe and pajamas and a cozy blanket —though Rory said she went rogue with the last one because she couldn't resist how soft it was.

See how nice they're all being?

And I was supposed to plant evidence on Chrissy's laptop.

To frame her for something she didn't do.

To *hurt* her.

When she did absolutely nothing to me.

Shit. I have to tell her—and do it now, while Pascal is here, while all the rest of them are too.

They deserve to know what kind of person they're sharing their space with.

Deserve to understand the shitstorm I'll likely bring into their lives.

I bend, reaching for the hem at my ankle where I sewed the flash drive before I left for the winery. A quick tug and it'll come free. I'd done that on purpose.

In and out.

Get into Chrissy's office, plug it into her laptop, transfer the files, get the hell out.

Let the powers that be do their thing.

But that *thing* had been a lot easier to swallow when I didn't really know her.

When she was just the spoiled daughter of a billionaire.

Not a woman who's passionate about helping animals and whose kind heart clearly expands to care about strangers she doesn't even know.

Dammit.

I have to tell them.

I open my mouth—

"You know your lips are still swollen."

"Rory!" Chrissy gasps, swatting her on the shoulder. "Don't say *that*."

Tiff sighs and shakes her head.

Marie's lips twitch but she just pulls out her phone and starts tapping at the screen.

"What? I mean, it's impressive, really. She's clearly a woman who's been thoroughly kissed and"—she leans closer, eyes flicking to the men where they're standing in the kitchen, deep in conversation—"I, for one, have always wondered what Brooks would be like when he kissed a woman."

Chrissy rolls her eyes. "Do I need to remind you that you *have* a husband?"

"No." She sighs dreamily. "King is a great kisser. But I'm curious by nature." A shrug. "So why can't I know if he's a kiss-you-senseless-because-he's-so-intense-he-can't-help-it or a slow-sip-you-up-until-your-bones-turn-to-goo kind of kisser?"

"Because it's none of our business?" Marie says dryly.

Tiff nods.

"Since when has that ever stopped us?"

Chrissy sighs heavily. "Rory—"

"He's both."

They freeze.

Then four gazes shoot to mine, four mouths falling open.

And somehow that encourages the words to flow.

"And," I yammer, "he's also a savor-until-your-heart-threatens-to-explode, and a gentle-*so*-gentle-your-eyes-well-up-with-tears, but my favorite is his"—oh God, why am I still talking?—"pin-you-in-place-and-fuck-your-mouth-with-his—"

"What are *we* talking about?"

My eyes go wide, cheeks burning—absolutely *burning*—when I realize the men have come near.

Far too near.

Near enough to—my stare drifts toward Brooks and I want nothing more than for the floor to open up and swallow me whole.

Because the heat in his eyes...

I know *exactly* what he's thinking.

He's *so* going to pin me in place and fuck my mouth with his tongue.

I shiver.

"Welp," Rory says, her mouth curving as her husband, King, draws her up to her feet and tucks her into his side, "I think it's time for us to head out."

"No," I say quickly, "that's okay—"

"Yes," Brooks says at the same time. "You should go."

"We should talk about the kittens," I blurt.

Chrissy's eyes come to mine...then flick over my shoulder and the edges of her mouth curve up. "I'll need to make some arrangements, so I'll be in contact later."

"*Much* later," Brooks mutters and I jump, not realizing how close he's come.

Smiles are smothered and looks are exchanged and then there's a flurry of activity as they all head for the door.

The *click* of the lock reengaging is the last thing I hear before silence descends.

Fingers trail over my nape and I don't flinch, don't jerk away. Instead, I shiver, fighting every instinct in me that says I should lean back into the touch.

Then I realize what's just happened.

What I didn't share.

"Wait," I say, rushing to the door. "We should call them back. I need—"

"Briar?" Brooks asks quietly.

My gaze jerks to his and the heat there...

Well, I'm certainly not thinking about a flash drive. Or framing an innocent woman for crimes she didn't commit.

I'm thinking it's been five years.

That the orgasm he gave me earlier did absolutely nothing to tamp down the need I have for him.

I'm thinking that I've missed him and that I understand why he did what he did.

I'm thinking I would have done whatever I had to in order to protect him back then.

And maybe I'm thinking that might still be true even after all this time.

"Baby," he murmurs and I jump again.

My eyes go to the door. "I need to tell them what I know."

"You told us enough for now," he says. "Pascal needs time to work, and you need some space to recover."

"I'm fine."

"Are you?"

There's something about his tone that lifts the hairs on my nape and I back up slowly, putting the couch between us. "Yes."

"Hmm." He moves to the door, fiddles with the handle.

"What are you doing?" I ask as he walks by me.

"Checking the locks." Then he does the same with the balcony doors.

But it's when he turns back toward me that my lungs seize.

Because the look in his eyes—

"So...do you still hate me?"

TWENTY-FIVE

BROOKS

SHE'S SO FUCKING CUTE, I want to kiss her.

But I need to know her answer to my question.

She lifts a hand and though part of me despises that it's trembling, I don't take my question back.

I just walk toward her.

And stay silent.

She nibbles at the corner of her mouth and looks away.

Which...pours icy cold water on the desire rippling through me, on my plans to kiss her senseless, to pin her against the wall and fuck her mouth with my tongue...to fuck other parts.

But her reply comes even as that frost is skating down my spine.

"No," she murmurs. "No." Her head comes up, eyes connecting with mine. "I tried to—so damned hard. And I hated what you did. Hated what you made me feel. Hated what you took away." She sighs, her gaze skating away. "But no, I don't think I ever truly hated you."

I exhale.

"And now—" She shakes her head.

"Now what?"

She's quiet for a long time, but I don't move, don't push. "Now, I guess...I understand. What it's like to be under that pressure, the way the fear grips you, how you never feel safe because the moment you let your guard down or think you've figured out a way to get clear of it...they'll make it obvious they're in charge. That they can get you anywhere."

"Not here," I rasp.

But I can't help the niggle forming in the back of my mind.

Because five years ago, they managed to get through every single roadblock I put in place.

Because even the nuclear option had resulted in—

Fuck.

I stumble back a step.

"Brooks." Her hand settles on my chest.

I shake my head, step back again. "Not here. I need to call Pascal, make sure that—"

"*Brooks.*"

"—he's taking the proper—"

Her arms come around me and before I can pull away, her body comes flush to mine and she hugs me. *Hard.*

"Shh," she whispers. "Just...breathe. We're here. We're safe. We're together."

And she's been through hell.

"How can I possibly fix what I did—what *they* did?"

Her arms band tighter, her forehead falling to my chest. She exhales and the warmth of her breath settles over me. "There's nothing for you to fix."

"Baby—"

She leans back. "There's *nothing* for you to fix."

"Bullshit."

"Does this mean you're going to brood instead of kiss me?"
I blink.

"Because I like all of your kisses, and earlier you reminded me exactly how much." Her lips tick up. "But I wasn't lying when I said I wanted another of your pin-me-in-place-and-fuck-my-mouth-with-your-tongue kisses."

I blink again.

"Though I'd also take a kiss-me-senseless-because-you're-so-intense-you-can't-help-it or a slow-sip-me-up-until-my-bones-turn-to-goo." She shrugs and I can't help it.

Even with all the shit that's happened, that's hanging over us, she still reaches a part of me that no one else ever has.

"You are so fucking beautiful," I whisper.

"You've told me that already." A lilting laugh. "And I'm not buying it." She tugs at the ends of her hair—which, admittedly —is a little rough around the edges. "Especially with this hack job."

"You'd be beautiful even if you were bald."

"And you're still too charming for your own good."

Something inside me untwists and a memory drifts to the front of my mind. "I seem to remember a certain someone who wouldn't give me the time of day when we first met."

"Well, okay, you were less than charming *that* day."

Laughter bubbles up. "You mean you didn't see me knocking your groceries out of your hands as the greatest form of flirting?"

"I really needed those eggs."

My smile fades. She had.

"Luckily you made it up to me." She steps close, lifts up on tiptoe, her eyes connecting with mine, *searching* mine. "So...are you going to make it up to me now?" A brush of her mouth over mine, her nails biting lightly into my shoulders. "Tonight?"

"We should—"

She kisses me.

And I stop thinking about all the mistakes I made, about all the ways everything went wrong.

All I can do is *feel*.

The softness of her lips against mine. The gentle curves of her body. The way her moan drifts through the air as I kiss my way along her jaw, down her throat.

Touching her earlier hadn't been nearly enough.

I need more. I *need* everything.

Lifting her into my arms, I carry her down the hall. But even as I'm walking, I can't stop kissing her, can't stop touching her.

Silky skin. Plump lips. Sleek tongue.

Her legs are around my waist and I can feel the heat of her even through the layers of our clothes. I know she'll be wet and hot, slick and tight.

Know she'll be mine.

Even with everything that's happened between us, all that still remains to be solved, that isn't going to change.

I won't let her go.

Not ever again.

She nips at my throat and I growl, dumping her on the mattress as heat arrows straight for my cock.

"Behave," I order.

Her mouth twitches. "But you really like it when I *don't* behave."

She's right.

I fell in love with the sweet girl with a spine of steel.

And then again with the woman who found joy in the journey, who never gave up, and who made it her life's mission to find out every single part of me—good or bad or in between...

And that included what I liked—and *really* liked—in bed.

Of course there wasn't anything I didn't like, not when it came to Briar's body and hands and mouth and *mind*.

She puts that gorgeous mind of hers to use, shoving me to my back and clambering on top of me.

I don't fight it—why would I when she's exactly where I want her to be...and when her hands are pushing my shirt up and she's bending, her lips coming to my skin?

Especially since I know she'll get distracted—okay, *I'll* distract her—and then she'll be misbehaving, but she'll be doing it with her pussy on my face and—

"Fuck!" I growl, so distracted by the thought of her sitting on my face that I missed her hand sliding down, dipping into my pants.

Wrapping around my cock and squeezing hard.

She just grins at me as she strokes.

And I know that Briar has done what she always does.

Turned the tables...

And I'm left just trying to keep up.

TWENTY-SIX

BRIAR

RIGHT.

So, getting my hands on Brooks's cock is probably not the smartest thing to do in this moment.

I should tell him to call the others back, should hand over the USB, should get the hell out...and none of those *shoulds* make the least bit of difference right now.

Because Brooks needs this.

Needs me.

Needs what I can give him.

And...I can't lie.

I want it too.

Hearing his groan in the air, feeling his body against mine. Desperate for the slight burn as he thrusts deep, the stretch and feeling of fullness from his cock, the hardness of him pressing into me. Our breaths mingling, our kisses intensifying until it's like we've become one person with a single pursuit.

Pleasure.

"Briar," he groans and I snap out of my memories, my fantasies.

Releasing his cock, I wrestle the button on his slacks open, tug down the zipper.

He's moving just as jerkily, yanking up my shirt, shoving down my pants.

"Wait," I say when he sweeps me up into his arms and he freezes.

Then he sets me on my knees beside him. "We can stop, baby." He cups my cheek. "Now. Later. Any time."

It's gentle, those words, that reassurance.

And hell, that spears through me.

And I know.

Know.

There's no way I'm coming out of this unscathed.

That even when I hated Brooks, I still loved him.

I've *always* loved him.

Even when I watched him walk away.

I close my eyes.

Then more *shoulds*—should stop, should leave, should keep him at a distance—

Ha.

How's that working for me?

I'm in my underwear and his pants are unbuttoned and I can still feel the imprint of his cock on my hand.

Something slides through his eyes when I peel back my lids but I don't let it process.

And I don't let him speak.

I just reach for the hem of his shirt and tug.

He watches me as he yanks it over his head, tosses it to the side.

"Now these," I order softly, pushing at the open waistband of his slacks.

Heat in his eyes as he obliges, but I know that he's watching closely. And I can't have that, can't let him know.

Why not? Why can't you start over? Why can't you have this?

I shove the questions from my mind.

Too late.

It's too late for us.

I've done too much, the gulf between us is too great.

But not too late for this, not too late for me to make him feel good.

Not too late for us to have a few more stolen moments before—

His slacks drop to the floor and then I'm really not thinking any longer. I'm shoving down his underwear and we're both groaning as I wrap my fingers around him and stroke.

Hard as steel. Soft as velvet. Hot as sin.

I want him in my mouth.

I want to feel him twitch as he comes in me, filling me up as I struggle to swallow him down.

But when I go to lower myself, he stops me.

"No, baby."

My eyes find his.

But he's looking away, brushing off my hand, pulling up his underwear.

My stomach twists and I reach for him again, but he just steps back, snagging his slacks and dragging them up his legs.

"I—"

He turns away and it's like a bucket of ice water has been dumped over my head.

I'm frozen as he moves to the bags, pulling out a pair of pajamas. He tears off the tags, tugs the top over my head and I robotically push my arms through the holes, steady myself on his shoulders as I put one leg into the pants, then the other.

"What are you doing?" I manage to ask.

"You think I don't see the look in your eyes?"

"I'm fine."

He just lifts his brows. "Bullshit."

I sigh. "Okay, so I *will* be fine as soon as you let me get my mouth on your cock."

More heat, but it's tempered now.

Shit.

I've messed this up.

"And I'll be *more* fine when you bend me over the couch and—"

His eyes lock with mine. "How about you level with me instead of trying to distract me with that gorgeous body?"

My heart starts pounding. "I've told you everything."

"Yeah?"

Except about the USB drive. I open my mouth—

"So what really happened when things got bad?"

My lungs seize. "Brooks."

"You lost your apartment—"

"I got another one." Eventually.

"You were alone with no money and no one to watch out for you and you yourself said things were bad. *Really* bad," he adds when I start to reply.

"It doesn't matter." I move to my pants, reach down and pick them up. "I need to tell—"

"Really bad," he repeats.

The memories try to creep in, but I put down a layer of ice to keep them sealed away. "Don't," I say through clenched teeth. "It's over. There's no point in going back."

"Like there was no point in thinking about your parents abandoning you? Or what your grandfather did to you? Or how you felt when *I* left?"

Phantom fingers wrap around my throat and start squeezing. "*Don't*," I rasp.

"You went through hell," he says. "Too many times, baby. And you can't keep shoving it down."

Rage loosens my throat. "I can do whatever the fuck I want."

"No, you can't."

"Who do you think you are to—"

"I'm the man who never stopped loving you."

I shake my head. "You left. I understand why," I add in a rush. "I probably would have done the same thing. But that was five years ago and things have changed—"

"None of the important things."

"That's bullshit and you know it."

"So says the woman who was just begging for my cock two minutes ago?"

"Temporary insanity," I mutter.

He steps close and gently cups my face in his hands. "Is it so bad that you don't want to tell me?"

No. I fucking don't want to tell him.

I don't want to think about it.

Definitely don't want to have a conversation about it.

"I thought you said you weren't going to pressure me to talk about it."

"That was before."

"Before what?"

"Before I realized you're still in love with me too."

TWENTY-SEVEN

BROOKS

HER LIPS PART ON A GASP. "That's not—"

"Don't try to lie to me, baby. It's always been that way, even when I was breaking your eggs," I snag the pants from her hands, drop them to the floor. "I loved you from that first day, and though it took me a bit to break through those thick, icy walls of yours, you fell for me then too. So talk to me. *Tell* me. Don't let the memories hold you hostage, don't use them against us, not now."

"There's no point."

"Why?"

"They probably already know where I am. And they're not going to stop until they get what they want." She shakes her head. "And if I don't give it to them, they'll…"

"They'll what?"

"The Lyons will hurt me or you or—" Her knees buckle. "Oh God! What if they target one of the others? Chrissy and Rome have a baby—"

"It's going to be okay. Jean-Michel says they're not particularly violent, and—"

"Not violent?" She shoves out of my arms. "Were they not *violent* when they lay in wait for me in my apartment and beat the shit out of me so I'd do a drop for them?"

"Baby—"

"Were they not violent when I ran and they tracked me down, dragged me back so I could pretend to be the girlfriend of a doddering old fuck they wanted to steal from?"

"Briar—"

"Don't worry, I didn't have to fuck him," she snaps. "But only because I swapped his Viagra with fake pills and he couldn't get it up."

I clench my hands at my sides.

Fuck. I need to punch something.

Some*one.*

"I didn't want to tell you because I knew you'd look at me like that, knew you think I'm..." She waves her hand. "I tried to ignore the letters—you know that doesn't work. And then I tried to fight them—newsflash, that shit didn't work either. So, I left. Again and *again* and every time I ended up right back here! With a disembodied voice on the other end of the phone telling me what to do. Only each time I was dragged back it was with more bruises, more scars."

The quiet that falls between us isn't silent.

Not in the least.

It's punctuated by our unsteady breathing, by the faint hum of the fan overhead, by the thundering of my pulse in my ears.

"How am I looking at you?" I ask long minutes later.

She turns away. "You know."

"Raindrop—"

Her body goes stiff and her words come sharp and icy.

"Like I'm dirty. Like I'm broken. Like I'm a leper who you won't ever want to touch again."

"Okay, now you're pissing me off."

She blinks.

"I want you more than I've ever wanted another woman. And I don't care who you fucked or touched."

A shake of her head.

"I hate that your choices were taken from you. I hate that you were forced to do things you didn't want to. And I hate that you were hurt, Raindrop. By me, by them, by the fucking shit they made you do. But I wouldn't care if you chose to fuck a hundred guys while we were apart." I move to pull her into my arms again, but when she steps away, I freeze. "I'd still love you. And I still won't let you go."

She's quiet, so damned quiet.

And Christ, I want to take her in my arms, *need* to hold her.

"Briar, baby?"

She shakes her head again, but doesn't retreat, thank fuck. Slowly, like I'm cornering a wild animal, I wrap my arms around her. It takes a long time for her to unfreeze, to relax into my touch.

"I didn't," she whispers.

"I don't care, Raindrop. I promise."

"I didn't," she whispers again. "The closest it ever came was that time. But one of the other women—" Her throat works. "Usually I worked alone, but sometimes there would be a few of us."

"She helped you?" I ask gently.

A nod. "Angela gave me the bottle of pills to swap out."

I stroke my hand up and down her back. "I'm glad."

Her forehead drops to my chest. "At first it was just dropping off things and picking them up or being a lookout. Then it was...more—playing a role, causing a distraction. But it's been escalating," she whispers. "Becoming riskier, like they don't care if I'm caught, like I'm dispensable."

"Good," I mutter.

She jerks in my hold. "Good?"

"It'll make it easier to get you out if they aren't trying so hard to keep you."

"Have you been listening to me at all? These people are dangerous!"

"Yeah, they are. So?"

Her mouth opens and closes, eyes flaring wide. "So we've both tried to fight them, but it didn't work."

"Anything else?"

Another flare of those gorgeous eyes. "What do you mean *anything else?*"

"I mean, is there anything else you haven't told me?"

"There are like five years of things, Brooks!" she snaps.

"Yeah," I say, "and I'm going to be here to listen to each and every one of them."

"You've lost your mind."

I smooth back her hair, something settling in me at the steel in her tone. "Maybe." I draw her closer. "But I'm not going to lose you."

"I don't know what we're doing."

"That's okay," I murmur. "I do."

She looks up, her eyes holding mine for a long, long moment. "I'm scared."

"I know. But this time is different."

"How? How can it possibly be different?" She sighs heavily. "They're always watching. Always ready to pounce."

"We have help," I remind her. "We're not keeping secrets." Something flashes across her eyes, but I keep talking before she can go back to arguing with me. "We're going to be okay."

"I don't think—"

"Then let's not think."

"Again"—she throws up her hands—"you've lost your mind."

"No. I lost *you* once and I can't do it again. But, baby, we also can't keep doing this, can't keep looking back and regretting all the things that went bad, worried about what might go wrong. We need to live for today, live for each other, live for what we can build together."

She closes her eyes and looks away, her words so quiet I can't discern them.

"What's that?"

A shake of her head.

"No more secrets, yeah?"

She sighs, and her eyes peel open.

But then she exhales and looks up.

And breaks my heart.

"I said, what happens when you leave again?"

TWENTY-EIGHT

BRIAR

I EXHALE and stare up at the ceiling.

I know what I said wasn't fair.

He'd explained.

I understood—under*stand*.

And I still brought it up in the way most designed to hurt him, to put distance between us.

Because he's right.

I love him.

I just...can't ignore the knot in my stomach, the knowledge that this isn't going to work out like he's planned.

It can't be that simple.

It *can't*.

But I also can't tell him no, not when he's so damned earnest, not when he's baring his heart. Not when he's making so much sense. And he's Brooks. The man who I trusted, befriended, loved...

Five years ago.

And—

"Dammit," I whisper, rolling over to my other side. He's right. I never stopped.

So I did the only thing I could.

Put a wall between us, widened that gulf.

Protected myself.

And now it's the middle of the night and I'm staring up at the ceiling and I'm trying to ignore the need nipping at my heels, telling me to get out of bed, to believe in him, in us.

To live for today because tomorrow may not be guaranteed.

So why don't I?

"Because I'm scared," I say, flopping to my back.

My life is a series of long, interminable straight roads followed by sharp, blind turns.

You'd think I'd be used to it—those sudden changes.

But I'm not.

I roll to my other side, sigh.

I'm scared.

Ugh.

I survived the last years—hell, I survived the childhood I had and now I'm scared of getting my heart broken again?

No. Well, yes. But also...I'm scared of Brooks getting hurt.

And Chrissy. And Pascal. And Jace. And the others.

I flop onto my back and groan.

Then I scrub my hands over my face and I know it's point-less to continue thinking in these endless circles. I need to do something—and that something isn't continuing to spin myself into a tizzy.

"Right," I whisper, sitting up and tossing the blankets to the side. "I need a plan."

So, I'll get the flash drive. Give it to Brooks and explain

what I was doing the night of the fundraiser. He'll pass it on to the others.

They'll probably be pissed and keep their distance.

But that's for the best.

It'll keep them far away from the shit show that's me.

Of course, they probably won't trust me with the kittens any longer, but that's for the best too.

No reason to put innocent creatures at risk.

I get out of bed, snag my pants from the floor, then creep toward the door, quietly turning the handle and stepping out into the hall. Dawn's just creeping over the horizon in the distance, casting the living room in a faint glow of light. But it's enough for me to make my way into the kitchen.

I snag a knife from the block and—

"What are you doing?"

Gasping, I whip around to see Pascal leaning against the wall, his arms crossed.

I clutch my pants and the knife to my chest, shame rippling through me.

I could pretend I was trying to leave. It might be easier than watching his face change.

But...that's not me.

Or not the me I want to be.

I use the knife to slice at the hem of my pants and pull out the drive. Then I take a breath and hold it out. "I was supposed to sneak in and put this in Chrissy's laptop the night of the fundraiser. I don't know exactly how it works, but I know enough. It contains software to install incriminating files on her computer." I find that he's suddenly right in front of me, his hand extended. I drop the flash drive into his hand and put the knife back. "I should have led with this. I was...well it doesn't matter what I was. Maybe there's some way to track it, to use it against them—"

He settles his hand on my shoulder, his eyes delving into mine. "Such shadows in you." A squeeze. "And such strength."

My lungs catch.

"But so little forgiveness." He turns away, stashing the drive in his pocket.

Heart squeezing. "I've forgiven Brooks," I say. "I understand why he did what he did."

"Not Brooks." His eyes come back to mine.

"I—"

But I don't finish the sentence.

Because he's still talking.

"For yourself, Briar."

Then, as I'm trying to absorb the blow of that, he disappears into the shadows.

I close my eyes and lean my head back against the wall.

The sun is up.

The day is beautiful.

Brooks came out of the guest bedroom an hour ago, looking like he slept about as well as I did.

Then he went into the office—needing to take some meetings in person.

He'd cupped my jaw before he left, brushed his lips over my forehead.

But I hadn't missed the hurt in his eyes.

"Ugh," I whisper, lifting my head and thunking it against the wall. "Why am I so messed up?"

"You know the cure for that, right?"

Shrieking, I lurch to my feet and stumble back, my gaze searching for a weapon.

The woman who's come out on the patio is a few years

older than me and pleasantly curved, her smile warm. But I'm not fooled. A threat can come from anywhere.

"Easy, sweetheart," she says.

"How'd you get in here?" I ask, moving toward the wrought iron chair. It's heavy and unwieldy for weapon purposes. But it's something.

Her brows pull together. "I used my key."

So much for Pascal's security.

I try to tell myself that's not a surprise—I knew they could get in anywhere at any time.

I just...wanted a little longer.

"What do you want me to do?" I ask.

I'm not going to do it.

No, I realize, the truth of that thought settling somewhere deep inside me, soothing an old wound...or maybe I'm just finally finding my spine, finding my will to live again. I'm not going to do what they want. Never again.

But it might help Brooks and Pascal if I could find out.

"Do?" The furrow between the woman's eyebrows deepens. "Umm...relax and"—her gaze drifts down my body and back up—"maybe eat something." My stomach rumbles, right on cue, and her lips curve. "Come on inside when you're ready and I'll make you something to eat."

She turns away, disappearing through the French doors, leaving me in the morning sunshine, the soft breeze buffeting my skin, the city spread out in front of me.

I hear the faint sounds of cooking through the glass.

Then the scents drift my way, making my stomach rumble again.

I peek inside, watch as the woman pokes through cabinets, pulls out ingredients.

"This is weird," I whisper.

She looks up as though she hears that and waves at me, gesturing for me to come inside.

And...

Hell, it's not like I'm going to jump off the balcony.

I might as well figure out what she really wants.

So, I release my death grip on the metal chair, take a deep breath, and go inside.

TWENTY-NINE

BROOKS

I'M ACUTELY aware of time inching by as I sit through my normal slew of Monday meetings.

They all feel unnecessary, but my assistant is really good at making sure I'm only at the ones I need to be at.

Decisions need to be made, connections need to be fostered.

But most of my brain—no, my *heart*—is at my apartment.

What happens when you leave again?

"That's all I have," Dan, my COO, says. "Do you have anything for me?"

I wrench my brain to the present, work my way through my list with Dan. "Any word on the buyout?" I ask as he starts packing up.

There was an attempt a few weeks back—another company trying to short our stock so they can come in and buy us out and take over.

It's a cowardly way to do business.

But it's not the first buyout effort I've thwarted.

If I sell—and I'd be hard-pressed to part with a business I built from the ground up, especially one that does work that is valuable and helps a lot of people—it won't be because I'm pressured into it.

"The rumors are swirling again."

"If they materialize into something concrete, let me know."

He nods, we exchange goodbyes, and I call Pascal, telling him about the rumors and the previous attempt at a buyout.

It may not be connected since I've fended off far too many of those.

But there's a niggling in the back of my brain that tells me these are all pieces of the same puzzle.

The drive, the buyouts, the sudden reappearance of Briar back in my life.

"Too much of a coincidence," I mutter.

"I agree," he says, and I expect him to hang up now that business is concluded. He's a busy man and always working on a dozen things at once. But today he lingers on the line. "When are you heading home?"

"Why?" I ask, alarm slicing through me. "Do I need—"

"She's fine," he says.

I exhale. "Then—" I break off.

He doesn't reply for several moments. Then he sighs. "I can't believe I'm about to do this shit."

"What shit?"

"Meddle," he mutters.

"I mean," I say as I recline back in my chair, "isn't that kind of your job?"

"I only meddle when it comes to personal safety," he grumbles. "Not with..."

"What?" I press.

"Not with shit that gets me involved in messy romantic situations."

I snort. Because I know that for the lie it is. Pascal has meddled with businessmen and hockey players and CEOs and stubborn fucks who refuse to get their heads on straight, alike.

"Just lay it on me so we can move on," I grind out.

"Briar needs a trauma therapist. And she needs space." A beat. "From you."

That smashes into me with all the gentleness of a train barreling down the tracks. "I told her I wouldn't walk away—not ever again."

And I won't.

We've hardly begun to fix what's wrong between us, but I can at least give her that much.

He sighs again, the sound rattling through the phone's speaker. "You're not seeing her clearly."

"I'm not seeing that she's been through hell and survived far too much?" I growl. "I fucking see it. I fucking hate it. But I also know she's been alone far too much in her life. She needs people around her, needs to know she's part of something, that people will have her back."

"With all due respect, she doesn't know anyone."

"She knows you."

"Barely."

"And Jace."

"And where were we when she was going through hell?"

"That's not on you guys."

A pause. "Maybe you're right," he says quietly. "Because it's on you."

Another collision, another truth slamming into me.

"Yes, it is." I force myself to take a deep breath. "And I'm glad that as fucked up as the last five years have been, you're still looking out for her, still trying to do what's best for her. I appreciate that. She *needs* that. But with all due respect, the last time I listened to you, I lost her for half a decade."

He lets the silence sit between us for long enough that a bolt of pain shoots through my jaw, it's ground together so tightly.

"Fine," he mutters. "I'll pass on information for trauma therapists. Make sure she sees one."

I open my mouth to reply, but he's already hung up.

"Christ," I mutter, scrubbing my hands over my face.

But even as I'm sitting in that, I hear the chime on my computer, know that my next call has started.

And again I'm supposed to somehow focus on work—in this case on earnings reports and where to put our R&D dollars—when the woman I love is hurting.

In danger.

With nothing resolved between us.

When a man I respect says I should stay away from her.

"Fuck," I whisper, but when there's a knock on the door and my assistant, Todd, pops his head in, I nod. "I'm hopping on."

He nods, disappears just as quickly.

As promised, I join the call.

I do it listening more than talking.

And when I do talk it's on topic and it's effective...even though half my brain is still thinking about Pascal's words.

The thought lingers as I trudge my way through the rest of my calls and on the drive home.

It nips at my heels as I take the elevator up, unlock the front door, all under the watchful eyes of Pascal's security team—most of whom I can't see, but can *feel* watching me.

Nape prickling, I push inside, still fighting with Pascal's words and the need tearing through me.

And the worry that he may be right.

That in order to save her, I may have to destroy any chance we have of a future together.

A future that, in a single glimpse of my living room, is laid out in front of me.

THIRTY

BRIAR

"SHH," I hear distantly. "She's sleeping."

"Not if you keep hissing like that."

Thunk.

"Not if *you* keep dropping things like *that.*"

"Both of you, quiet down and come into the kitchen. I have some cookies that are fresh out of the oven."

Footsteps recede as I take stock of where I am and what's happening around me.

Brooks's apartment.

Delicious scents in the air—that's not a surprise, they've been filling my nose from the moment I walked in off the balcony.

River introduced herself, and I don't know how I didn't put the pieces together right away, what with her cooking and cleaning and having her own key, and Pascal's security not stopping her from accessing the apartment, but it didn't take long to relax to her presence. She's definitely related to Dolores

—a total sweetheart and her food is fabulous, and her constant chattering as she buzzed around the space was both comforting and amusing. Especially when she griped about Brooks never being in town to eat her cooking.

"Stock my freezer," she said in a voice that sounded hilariously close to Brooks's own. "I'll just nuke it whenever I'm hungry. *Nuke* it!" She'd tossed up her hands. "Does he not know how hard it is to make the breadcrumbs crispy?"

"Probably not," I told her when she paused, clearly waiting for my reply.

A disgusted sound as she vigorously wiped down the kitchen. "You're certainly right."

"So, what did you do?" I found myself asking into the quiet.

She scowled. "I created recipes that could be frozen." A scowl. "Then *nuked.*"

My lips twitched, and though I tried to help, I found myself relegated to the couch and chattered at.

Which was...nice, even though she was talking about people I didn't know, things I didn't one hundred percent understand. We did, however, bond over the excellent cleaning abilities of baking soda and lemon juice and the frustration that dust bunnies always seemed to appear immediately after sweeping the floor.

I tried to remember what happened after that, but it comes up fuzzy, and embarrassment heats my cheeks as I peel my eyes open.

Clearly I fell asleep in the middle of our conversation and missed...

A *lot.*

The living room is transformed.

A huge cat tower sits next to the fireplace and I can almost imagine the foster kittens climbing it so they can teeter across the mantle, bat at the television screen while a Grizzlies (or, cough, Eagles considering Jean-Michel, Rome, and King's—and their women's—loyalties) game plays in the background.

Beds are placed strategically around, along with carriers and little houses that provide space for the kittens to hide.

There are a couple of small water fountains, food dishes, and litter boxes cleverly disguised as side tables...

And a toy-plosion.

It's like a pet store took over while I was sleeping.

Just without the kittens.

Frowning, a coil of disappointment sliding through me, I sit up and look around.

But not a single fluff ball is in sight.

"Oh, you're up," I hear and turn to see Chrissy, Rory, and River sitting in the kitchen, each with a steaming mug in front of them.

"*You* woke her up." River scowls. "I told you two you should come back."

"We made a dozen trips right by her over the last hour and she didn't so much as move," Rory says. "I think she's fine."

"I am." I stand and stretch.

"Still," Chrissy murmurs, coming over to me and giving me a quick hug. "We're sorry we woke you. Rome is watching the baby and King is bringing the kittens over in just a bit, so we were on a bit of a time crunch."

"They going to be here soon?"

Her face goes soft and I know it's because the eagerness in my question is obvious.

But I can't help it.

Kitties!

Despite seriously resenting working on the farm growing up, I got used to having animals around. Years ago, Brooks had offered to fill our house with critters, the stables with horses, but at first, I just wanted to breathe. Then when I started school and he was sweeping me off to spend time with him in fabulous locations on my days off, I knew I couldn't give a pet the time they deserved, so I held off.

Now, though, I have nothing *but* time.

I'm stuck in this apartment with nothing to do. So why not cuddle some adorable little fluffer nuggets?

Well, I don't actually *have* to stay. I could leave. Could go back to my life.

I'm just...I'm not quite ready to go yet.

A soft knock pulls me out of those depressing thoughts and a man I don't recognize pops his head in through the front door, sending my pulse skittering.

"Hey, John," Chrissy says, and I relax when it's clear she knows him. "Everything okay?"

He nods then pushes the door open further, holding it for... Kittens!

Their tiny meows reach my ears before I realize that another man is behind King, two additional carriers in hand. He's tall, with salt and pepper hair, but he hefts the carriers with ease.

"Thorn!" Chrissy exclaims, hurrying over and taking one of the containers from him. "You didn't have to help."

He shrugs. "What else am I gonna do when I walk by and see the man struggling?"

I can think of a lot of things—namely, what most people would do.

Walk by and carry on with their day.

But he hadn't, and that along with the careful way he brings the kennel over, sets it on the floor, tells me all I need to know about him.

He's scowly and his tone borders on sharp. But he's good.

"Can I get you guys anything?" River asks, coming over and all but shoving a mug of hot cocoa in my hand.

But her eyes aren't on me.

They're on Thorn.

Hmm.

"No, thanks. I need to head back to the office," he murmurs.

But I don't miss the way his eyes linger on River right back.

Double *hmm.*

"Really?" Chrissy says, obviously disappointed as she bends and opens the door to one of the carriers. "We were all going to stay for dinner—and no, that's not a dinner you're going to cook." She smiles at River. "Rome and my dad are bringing food."

Protest flashes across River's face. "I couldn't possibly—"

"Yes, you could," Rory says, linking her arm through River's.

"No—"

"Oh, honey. I—"

"Sweet mother of Christ!" Thorn shouts.

Right as the front door swings open again.

THIRTY-ONE

BROOKS

THE SHOUT HAS me bustling forward...then promptly screeching to a halt as I fight a smile.

Thorn—surly, grumpy, taciturn *Thorn*—Wilkenson is jerking like he's being electrocuted, arms and legs shooting out to the sides, back bending in odd angles, curses raining from his lips as a tiny ball of white fluff crawls up his body.

Calf. Thigh. Hip. Back...

The ball of fluff doesn't stop moving until it's settled itself on Thorn's shoulders.

"Meow!"

Hell if that isn't a cry of victory.

The room is silent, the girls looking at each other with wide eyes and smothered smiles.

Thorn is glaring down at his shoulder—though it has to be noted that he hasn't made a move to dislodge the interloper.

"Should I?" Briar asks, stepping toward him.

Chrissy loses her fight with her smile. "I think Thorn has been claimed."

Thorn glares at her...but still doesn't remove the critter. Instead, he nods at Briar. But when she tries to lift the kitten off him, the kitten digs its claws, making him curse again.

"I...uh..."

"I think this means he's staying for dinner," Rory says, her mouth curving up.

"No—"

But there's a knock behind me and the next ten minutes are a flurry of unpacking the food Jean-Michel and Rome have brought, releasing the rest of the kittens from Kitty Jail and the baby from Car Seat Lockup, the arrival of Jace and Marie, and finally convincing River to sit down and take a break for a change.

Through it all Thorn doesn't move.

And neither does the kitten.

My lips twitch as Chrissy offers him a plate. He takes it with a scowl, jabbing his fork into the pasta and salad.

"Here."

I turn, see that Briar is standing beside me.

The dark circles beneath her eyes are softer, the sharp edges on her face from not having enough to eat already gentling. River is working her magic.

"Thanks," I say softly, taking the plate she's holding.

A nod before she turns away.

"Briar?"

Her eyes come back to mine. "You okay?"

She nibbles at her bottom lip. "I'm fine."

My mouth hitches up and though I expect her to walk away, she pauses, her brows coming up. "Why are you smiling?"

"I'm just thinking that some things never change."

She frowns.

I lean in, brush my thumb over the V that's formed. "You always say you're fine. Aliens could be invading and the human race at risk of extinction and you'd still say you were fine."

Her nose wrinkles. "I want to argue with you."

"*That's* new," I quip when it's clearly not.

The Briar of the past was beyond sweet, yes, but she was also tough as nails when something really mattered, and once I made my way past those thick, icy walls of hers and she trusted me, she hadn't shied away from making her wishes known.

I expect her to glare at me.

Instead, she smiles.

"What?" I ask.

"I'm remembering that time on the island."

Warm sand. Crystal blue water. Waves lapping at our toes, the sun setting in the distance, and...Briar yelling at me.

Our first argument ever.

"I don't even remember what we were fighting about," I say, daring to move a little closer.

Her eyes flare...exactly as they had on that beach. "Seriously?"

"I feel like it had something to do with you being completely unreasonable—"

She gasps in outrage, smacks my arm. "I was *so* not being unreasonable. You were being your typical pushy, billionaire self, and I was just trying to cook a meal."

"You kicked the chef out of the kitchen so you could take over."

"I gave her the night off because she'd been working so hard!"

"And then rearranged her kitchen," I say dryly.

Her eyes narrow. "I was just organizing."

"So she couldn't find anything?"

"Excuse me for—"

Someone clears their throat and Briar and I freeze. Slowly, I tear my gaze from her beautiful face and remember...

We're not alone.

And everyone is watching us.

There are smiles all around—on every face except for Thorn, that is.

But he's not scowling, which is a freaking miracle in and of itself.

"Here's your plate," Chrissy says brightly, bringing it over to Briar.

"Thanks."

The quiet stretches for a moment before Rory says something outrageous, making everyone laugh as they eat. Then Chrissy's baby starts crying and Rome jumps in with diaper duty while she preps a bottle. King and Jean-Michel start discussing the team's upcoming road trip game while River fusses over everyone—though she at least makes her way through her own plate as she buzzes about.

It's chaotic and loud and it's far from the first time I've been swept up in the whirlwind of people that Jace brought into my life.

At first, it was weird, overwhelming.

Then it became like home.

But is Briar feeling the same?

Or is she—a woman who's spent far too much time alone—stuck in overwhelm like the other day?

My gaze keeps going to her, watching, waiting for any sign this all might be too much. But though she's quiet and subdued, sitting on the floor next to the giant ass cat tower that now dominates my living room, a pair of kittens in her lap, she seems relaxed.

She absently pets the cats, her mouth curved into a small smile as she takes in the craziness that's become my normal.

"You okay?"

I turn to Jace, though it's remarkably hard for me to tear my gaze from Briar. "I'm not the one who's been through a nightmare."

His eyebrows lift. "Haven't you?"

"I shouldn't have walked away," I mutter. "This shit is all my fault."

"I think this *shit* is much deeper than any of us realize— Jean-Michel's ex showing up after everyone thought she was dead and creating a nightmare for him and Chrissy, not to mention all that shit with Cam and Attie—"

Cam plays for the Eagles and his wife is an FBI agent who was shot during the investigation of Jean-Michel's ex and a group of human traffickers linked to the Lyons.

"—not to mention the attacks on our companies and the blackmail and letters and everything that happened with Briar."

I blink. "You think it's all connected?"

"Do you somehow think it's *not*?"

"I didn't even know Jean-Michel until you started working with him," I hedge, though somehow, I know he's right.

"And when was that?"

I still, start thinking back. "About three months before you began your first project with him. So you're saying..." But I trail off because I don't *know* what he's saying. The connection is Jean-Michel or Jace or none of us and we have no clue what the fuck is really going on?

"I'm saying there's more here than we understand. And Thorn isn't immune either, his company was the victim of corporate espionage a few months back and some investors have been trying to take over the board." He shakes his head.

"Me. You. Thorn. Jean-Michel. We've all dealt with attacks on our companies—though you and Jean-Michel are the only ones whose attacks were personal. I don't know if it's because Thorn and I didn't have anyone important in our lives when we were targeted or if it's deeper than that. I just know my instincts are screaming that *all* of this shit is connected."

I open my mouth to reply—to *agree*—but I don't get the chance to.

Because Pascal is suddenly in front of me.

"We need to talk."

THIRTY-TWO

BRIAR

CHRISSY HAS her baby in one arm, a kitten in the other.

It's beautiful and she catches me watching her.

"You want to hold her?"

"Sure."

But when I reach for the kitten, she shakes her head with a smile and shifts her sleeping daughter out of her arms.

"Are you sure—" I don't get to finish the question because Mia is suddenly in my lap, her head cradled in the crease of my elbow and...

I'm in love.

The soft weight of her tiny body in my arms. The scent of baby filling my senses. The way her nose crinkles as though she knows, even in sleep, that I'm not her mama.

"She is absolutely gorgeous," I say quietly, gently stroking a finger down her button nose.

"Mother's bias"—Chrissy grins—"but I happen to agree with you."

And the guilt ramps again.

Here Chrissy is with kittens—and yes, I know that I'm helping out by having agreed—sort of—to watch the fluffy babies, but I also have the feeling that she only offered because she knew I needed to do something that wasn't just sitting in this apartment, worrying about what my future might look like. So, kittens and arranging for dinner and being so kind and inclusive. *All* of them have been making sure I'm included in the conversation.

And now she's trusting me to hold her baby.

Dammit, I'm an asshole.

"Chrissy," I begin.

"Uh-oh," Rory says.

I close my eyes, exhale. "I need—"

"I know." She reaches forward and squeezes my hand. "I remember you from the night of the fundraiser—or your eyes, anyway."

"They really are striking," Rory agrees. "And that hair of yours is uniquely beautiful, though the ends are *tragic*."

"Rory!"

Marie types on her phone from beside me. "You know you have no hope of corralling that mouth of hers, so why do you even try?"

Chrissy scowls. "Because at some point I hope to slap some manners into her."

"That might require an actual *slap*," Marie points out.

"Rude," Rory grumbles.

"What?" Marie shrugs. "I'm not entirely convinced that you're trainable, but Chrissy seems determined to keep trying."

Tiff bites her lip. "I don't think this is an appropriate conversation considering..." Her eyes flick to me and her words trail off.

Rory bumps her shoulder against Tiff's. "It's okay, buttercup," she says, borrowing Jean-Michel's nickname for his wife. "I've done the work and I know my besties would never actually try to slap some sense into me." Her gaze comes to mine. "The elephant in the room sweet Tiff is trying to avoid is that my ex was abusive."

Rage coils in my belly in a sudden rush. "He *what?*" Someone tried to dim the beautiful spirit of this woman?

"Whoa, Tiger," Rory says, her hand settling on my knee. "I'm okay. Truly. I've had a lot of therapy and I found someone"—her eyes slide to King—"who loves me and makes sure I know it."

"I'm glad."

"What about you?" she murmurs. "Have you had therapy?"

I rock back slightly. Is it that obvious I'm fucked up?

She squeezes my knee. "I don't mean to be pushy—"

Marie snorts.

Rory glares but goes on. "But it's clear you've been hurt and I have a killer recommendation for a therapist—"

My gaze flies to Brooks. "He didn't—"

"He *did*," Marie interjects quietly.

"Fine," I say. "He hurt me—not physically, of course. And I know he thought he was doing it to protect me, so how can I be mad?"

"Because you're normal?" Rory asks. "And because it seems like a lot has changed in a short amount of time and you probably don't know how to process it?"

I nibble at the inside of my mouth.

She's not wrong.

But I hurt him too.

Not *just* physically.

I stole from him, turned over incriminating information to people who don't hesitate to dish out pain. And I know he says he's not worried, that the stuff on there doesn't directly involve him, just shit his dad did, I know it can't be that simple.

They wouldn't have wanted it so badly if it didn't have the power to hurt him.

"We don't have to talk about this," Tiff says.

I smile at her, though I know it's a facsimile of my normal one. "Thanks. I'm okay. I'm just...I guess I don't actually know *what* I am."

"Fair," Rory says with a laugh. "I think we've all been there."

"And you guys are being so nice—*too* nice." I turn to Chrissy. "Especially after I crashed your event and was supposed to..."

Rory lifts her eyebrows. "To..."

My stomach starts to twist but I can't form the words.

Chrissy touches my arm. "Pascal told me."

"Told you what?" Rory asks, protectiveness bleeding into her tone.

Because as welcoming as these women have been to me, they're a unit, they've taken the time to build trust with each other.

I'm just an outsider.

Who conspired to hurt Chrissy.

Guilt churns through me.

"I know," Chrissy murmurs. "You don't have to explain further."

"You know?" I ask.

"You told Pascal. He told my dad." A shrug. "My dad told me."

"And me," Tiff adds.

"I know, too," Marie says.

"You mean..." I blink as I look around the room, as I

remember all the things they said and did. They knew and they still welcomed me like—

"What. The. *Hell?!*"

My eyes whip toward Rory.

"You mean you all know something that *I* don't know?"

Chrissy winces. "It wasn't my story to share, Ror."

"Except with Marie and Tiff and Jean-Michel and *you*."

"Honey, I—"

"I crashed the party because they ordered me to sneak into Chrissy's office and plant files on her computer," I blurt. "It wasn't that big of a deal—I mean the sneaking in part. I just watched for a little while and put a disguise together then pretended to be part of the serving staff. All I did was check coats."

They stare at me.

"At least until Brooks caught up with me."

More staring.

"And I mean, the planting the files thing is bad—*really* bad. I know that. But it's not as bad as what I did to Brooks—"

"What did you do to Brooks?" Marie asks quietly.

More guilt, so much guilt that the words keep coming even though I need to just stop *talking*. "I broke into his house and..." I tell them about the window and the guards and sneaking into his office, using my knowledge of the space to get into the safe. I tell them of the struggle, of getting away with the incriminating information about his dad. "I hurt him," I whisper. "He still has a bit of a bruise on his temple and he was almost unconscious when I left." My voice breaks. "My childhood was violent and these last few years...I never thought I would be like *them*. That I'd get physical and hurt someone. But in his office, I was desperate and —" I sigh. "And I was so freaking *mad* thinking that he was living this great life after leaving me at the altar when I was..."

"In hell," Marie finishes.

"He left to protect me," I say in a hurry. "But I didn't know that until a couple of days ago, so emotions were high and..." I groan. "It was a mess."

Chrissy sighs. "A bit more than a mess, I think."

"Yeah."

Tiff squeezes my knee.

We all fall silent.

For a few moments anyway.

"That. Is. *So*. Cool!" Rory exclaims making baby Mia jump in my arms, though she doesn't wake up, thankfully. "I mean, not about the whole framing for a crime or whatever thing." She waves a hand dismissively. "I'm sure JM and Pascal would have cleared that right up, regardless. But you're a total badass, Briar. You bested Brooks *and* infiltrated Chrissy's event in a disguise—"

"I got caught," I remind her.

"Eh," she says. "That was for the best. You're here now and you got a sexy Brooks for your trouble."

I force a smile, but my eyes drift across the room—right to the objectively sexy Brooks.

His eyes come to mine and my pulse starts skittering through my veins.

"Right." Marie puts her phone away. "I think maybe that's our cue to go."

"No way," Rory exclaims. "We're finally getting to the good stuff."

Chrissy sighs.

Tiff hides a smile.

"And now we're getting back to Rory being impossible to train," Marie says dryly.

I tear my eyes from Brooks and watch as Chrissy wrinkles

her nose. "I know, but what can we do?" she says. "I've already tried positive reinforcement."

"Seriously?" Rory snaps.

"Did I or did I not help you devour an entire bag of peanut M&Ms last week?"

"If by devour, you mean *you* ate most of the bag, then yes."

A gasp of outrage. "You had at least half."

"Did not."

"Did *too*."

"I'm breastfeeding"—Chrissy's chin comes up—"my body needs extra nutrition."

"I don't think M&Ms count as *nutrition*."

"They have peanuts in them. That's protein."

Rory snorts. "Should we ask the Eagles' nutritionist to weigh in on that?"

Marie looks up from her phone and winks at me. "I'm thinking they *both* could use some training."

My mouth twitches and I'm about to chime in when I realize that our group has suddenly grown by one.

Pascal is standing next to Brooks.

And he looks...

THIRTY-THREE

BROOKS

"MEOW!"

I look down at my feet, see the kitten that Thorn had claimed—or that had claimed Thorn. Its accusing eyes pierce into mine. "Don't look at me," I mutter. "He's the one with the heart of ice who left you behind."

"Meow!"

Sighing, I bend over and scoop her up. "Don't worry," I murmur. "I'm sure he'll cave to your theatrics soon enough."

Thorn might be a surly bastard, but the careful way he'd handled the kitten betrayed him.

Violet—the litter is named after flowers this time—will be on her way to her permanent home soon enough.

And that home will be with Thorn.

"How long do you give it, huh?" I stroke my hand along her little back. "A week? Nah. I give the man two days before he caves."

"Meow!"

"I know. But I've got you while you wait. You can claw the furniture, run like a maniac through the halls, and fill that little belly with kitty kibble."

"Meow!"

"And you'll wear down Grump McGrumperface soon enough. He'll spoil you rotten."

"Meow."

"Yeah, he's grumpy, but he's a good guy. He'll treat you right."

"Meow." She stretches, rubbing her face against my chin. "Meow. Meow. Meow."

"Okay, Ms. Chatterbox," I murmur, walking her over to her siblings and settling her near one of the fluffy beds that have taken over my living room. She immediately starts batting at a feather-encrusted ball, drawing her two brothers' and three sisters' attention. A Kitty Royale for domination of the feather ball ensues and I find myself watching the chaos and smiling.

I should be freaking out.

Should be frantically trying to fix this.

Pascal's crew had intercepted a letter.

It was a photo of Briar and me leaving the charity function, my fingers wrapped tightly around her arm, our faces angry.

No note with it.

No threat.

Just a clear message that they're watching.

Who exactly is watching, we don't know. Though Pascal has tracked down a link confirming that Jace is right. It seems like this shit is all connected.

The Lyon family is the scum of the earth.

(And, joy, my father worked closely with them).

So, it's not just the personal attacks on me and Jean-Michel and Chrissy, nor even the corporate espionage and under-handed tactics within all our companies.

It's not what they did to Briar.

It's all of that...*plus* human trafficking and God knows what else.

Attie, the FBI agent in charge of the investigation that brought down part of their human trafficking ring last year, knows there are other arms of the organization she hasn't uncovered yet, but they seem to be able to slip in and out of the corporate world and the dark underbelly of the crime world with equanimity.

She said they're like a fucking hydra—cut off one head and another emerges.

Fucking Lyons.

But even though Pascal had imparted that information before heading back out to do security chief things, I feel remarkably...steady?

It doesn't make sense.

Except that Briar is here.

We have a second chance to figure this shit out together.

And Rory passed along the name of her trauma therapist before she left, along with a whispered word saying she'd already booked Briar an appointment for the next day.

Presumptuous.

But effective, I have to admit.

The kittens scatter and I turn to see Briar standing in the hall. Her skin is flushed pink and she's wrapped in a robe, her hair bundled on the top of her head. "Hey," she says softly.

"Hey."

And...cue awkward silence.

"You tired?" I ask softly.

"I thought I was."

"But now?"

"My mind is going a thousand different directions."

"Want to talk about it?"

She sighs, tucks a piece of her hair behind her ear. "No." Her mouth hitches up. "I'm tired of talking."

"Want to watch a movie?"

Her face goes soft. "Which movie?"

"You pick."

"Really?"

"It's your turn."

We always switched off, and, five years ago, during our last movie night together, I made the selection.

Her brows drag together as she processes that. "God, that's right. You chose that awful action flick."

"It wasn't awful."

Now those brows fly up. "Really? *That's* what you're going with?"

"The fight scenes were epic."

"And improbable." A beat. "With CGI from the eighties."

My lips twitch but I just pass her the remote then head for the kitchen to make popcorn. By the time I'm coming back, a bowl in my hands, she's made a choice.

One has me stifling a groan.

The Princess Bride, really?

We must have watched it a hundred times together.

Her eyes come to mine and there's something clinging to their edges that makes my heart ache. Like she's extended an olive branch but some part of her is waiting for me to bat it away.

Instead, I wrap my fingers around it, cradle it close to my chest.

Then I pass her the popcorn, murmur, "As you wish."

THE LAST THING I remember is fleeing the Fire Swamp—

No, it was Buttercup and Wesley fleeing the horrors of that treacherous swamp.

So why does it feel like I'm navigating something equally as risky?

Probably because Briar is sleeping on my chest, her face peaceful and young, and for a moment, I can pretend I've gone back in time, back before all this shit happened.

I gently smooth my hand over her hair, the strands like silk.

Though not as soft as the fur from the two kittens curled up next to her.

They start purring as I pet them and I know that Briar and I have been claimed the same as Thorn.

The only question is if Briar's going to let me claim her too.

I turn off the TV, carefully extract us from the pile of kittens, and carry Briar down the hall. The door's closed because Chrissy advised us to limit the parts of the apartment the kittens will have access to, but it sure as shit makes it difficult for me to get in the bedroom with my woman in my arms.

Eventually, I manage to turn the knob, get her through the door, and then onto the bed, all without waking her.

I tug the blankets up, turn for the hall.

"Brooks?" I hear as I reach the threshold.

She's rumpled and sleepy, her hair tumbling down her shoulders.

"Yeah, baby?"

"I used to think the fantasy was the fact that you swept in and rescued me from the disaster that was my life."

My heart starts pounding.

"But I've learned that the fantasy is actually the small things. Popcorn and a movie. A purring kitten and hot chocolate. Spending time with friends and warm arms keeping me safe."

My pulse is thrumming through my veins so rapidly I feel lightheaded.

It's all I can do to stay on my feet.

Let alone come up with something to say in response.

She takes care of that for me.

"Goodnight, Brooks."

But as I walk down the hall to my office, all I can think of is Pascal's words.

She needs space. From you.

And how much of a monster it makes me if I can't give her that.

THIRTY-FOUR

BRIAR

"MEOW. MEOW. MEOW-MEOW-MEOW!" My lips twitch as I glance down at Tulip. She lifts up on her back legs, rubs her face against my leg.

"I'll scratch you in a minute," I murmur. "Right now my hands are dirty."

I'm making bread.

Yup.

Bread.

It's been two weeks since that night at the winery and I haven't left this freaking apartment.

Because Pascal says it's not safe yet.

I've met with a therapist three times. The first was because Rory showed up with a laptop and logged me on to the virtual visit before leaving the apartment.

The next two were because I found it to be helpful.

Look, I'm not a stunted adult trapped in my childhood.

It was shit. It was abusive. It was wrong. I had plenty of time on my own to understand that much.

Does it make sense to me?

No.

Do I understand why my parents, why my grandfather couldn't love me?

No.

What did I do wrong? Why wasn't I enough?

Lots of big feelings and old hurts and things I wish I could pretend didn't still bother me.

The only piece that makes sense, the doesn't hurt like it once did, is...Brooks. I understand why he did what he did. It makes sense. I would have done the same thing to protect him.

All that matters is that he's back now and I've decided to stay and, aside from the fact that we haven't kissed since that night a few weeks ago, I have my best friend back.

"Meow!"

"Almost ready, Tulip," I say as River bustles into the room.

"How's it coming, sweetheart?" she asks.

And maybe this woman—along with the rest of the family that Brooks has built over the last five years—is part of why I feel okay, even though I spent ninety minutes this morning unpacking emotional baggage with my therapist.

Because River has been here every day.

At first I thought it was because that was her job, to be here every day. It felt like overkill—even with the kittens, Brooks and I didn't make that much of a mess, and it's not like there isn't plenty of food in the house. Then I realized she only appeared when Brooks had to go into the office.

And I knew it was a silent message from Brooks to me.

He's not leaving me alone, not ever again.

Hot cocoa and movie nights. Popcorn and *The Princess*

Bride. Dinners and breakfast together and...Brooks carrying me to bed every single night.

Us.

Albeit without kisses or other reminders that "our time hasn't passed."

Nothing except time together.

Which is a good thing. It's allowing us time to rebuild the trust between us, to learn each other as we are now.

Even if my body is—

"You okay, honey?"

I jump as a hand settles on my back and the bowl teeters on the edge of the counter. "Shoot," I hiss, reaching for it.

But River is reaching too and we bump into each other, both of us missing the catch.

The bowl crashes to the ground, sending dough in every direction.

Unbidden, my eyes well with tears. "Dammit," I whisper.

"Oh, sweetheart. I'm so sorry."

I shake my head. "It's my fault. When someone touches me when I don't expect it—" My throat goes tight and I crouch down to start cleaning up the mess. "It's been getting better"—especially with Chrissy and Rory and the others around as often as they've been—"but I wasn't paying attention. I'm sorry I ruined the bread."

"*Tsk.* It's not ruined. This recipe only takes a second to throw together." She rights the bowl, scoops the remnants inside, and puts it back onto the counter. Then sits down beside me.

I sigh, scrub at my eyes.

She lifts a hand, slowly, making sure I see it, and my heart kicks hard even as shame ripples through me. She's so damned nice and I'm so fucked up. Her fingers brush mine and then she guides me down so we're both sitting on the floor, our backs against the cabinet.

This close, I can see the gold specks in her rich chocolate eyes. Her skin is...perfection. A few faint lines around her eyes and mouth, across her forehead, making it clear to the world that she smiles regularly, and she positively glows with vigor, her complexion all peaches and cream, the deep brown of her hair the perfect complement—even with the few strands of gray in the mix.

"You're beautiful," I blurt and her cheeks go pink.

She waves a hand. "Oh, honey. Those years are far behind me."

"What are you? Thirty-five?"

A chuckle. "Now you're just pulling my leg. I'm a decade older than that, love. But thank you for being so sweet."

I'm not being sweet.

It's the truth.

But it's also me going for a distraction so I don't have to delve into all of the ways I'm so fucked up.

"We should remake—"

Her fingers squeeze mine. "Wait just a second, sweetheart."

And, dammit, there my eyes go again.

She sees them, reaching into her pocket and passing me a packet of tissues.

"Thanks," I whisper, dabbing at the corners of my eyes. "And again I'm sorry."

"No more apologies." She sighs and leans back against the cabinets. "It gets better, you know."

I still. "What gets better?"

"Being scared all the time. Jumping when someone surprises you." A beat. "Thinking that touch can only be laced with pain."

"River," I begin.

"I thought I had to be perfect, thought if I just did things exactly the way he preferred then he'd keep his fists to himself." She looks away and this time, I find that I'm the one who's reaching across the space between us to offer comfort. "But it didn't matter how hard I worked or how perfect I was, the abuse didn't stop."

I suck in a breath and nod.

"I got out." An exhale. "And he dragged me back. Then I got out again and again and again, and every single time I ended up right back in that house."

"Oh, River."

"All that matters is that I'm not there any longer." She squeezes my hand and pulls back. "And I know it's not what you went through. I'm only telling you so that you know I understand, at least a little bit."

"I think you understand *exactly* what I'm feeling."

"Maybe," she murmurs.

"Definitely."

"Okay then." A breath. "So you need to know it gets better. Trust that there are good people in this world." She touches my cheek. "And trust that you'll be able to find them."

"I know that's true."

"Yeah?" Hope blazes in her gorgeous eyes.

"Yeah," I tell her. "Because you're in my life now."

Her eyes fill with tears but her smile is as beautiful as she is. "Just try and get rid of me."

"Never." I climb to my feet, extend a hand to help her to hers. "Now should we attempt Bread 2.0?"

"I think—" But she freezes, as though something catches her focus.

I follow her gaze and warmth floods me as I see Brooks standing just a few feet away, his expression unfathomable.

Before I can process that, I realize there's someone behind him.

Thorn.

And the rage in *his* expression is unending.

THIRTY-FIVE

BROOKS

I WAS surprised when Thorn asked to meet up at my place, though him showing with a bag of completely unnecessary cat toys wasn't exactly shocking.

He's been claimed.

Violet will be old enough to be adopted in the next week.

The only question is if Thorn will get over himself enough to bring the kitten home with him.

I nod toward the security guard on duty, unlock the door, and push inside.

There's a crash and I rush forward, but even before I'm recognizing it's just a minor mishap in the kitchen, River and Briar's voices reach me.

And I'm eavesdropping—*we're* eavesdropping.

But I can't make myself stop.

Neither, it appears, can Thorn.

He tenses, face going stonier than I've ever seen. He doesn't interrupt, though.

And neither do I.

Not when Briar's voice breaks, nor when River shares something I never knew, not even as they both bond over the fucked-up-ness that's shadowed their lives.

It's only as they stand that I realize we should have stepped out.

Or at least have made it so they didn't realize we were blatantly listening in.

Too late, though.

"Um, hey," Briar says, her cheeks pink as she tucks a strand of hair behind her ear. "I didn't hear you come in."

I open my mouth—

"Meow!"

Violet to the rescue.

She sprints across the room, bypassing me completely, and—

"Ow, shit. Fuck. *Ow!*" The bag hits the hardwood and then Thorn is peeling the kitten from his thigh. But he does it gently, almost as gently as he cuddles her close and settles her on his shoulder. "You're a pain in the ass," he mutters to the cat.

"Meow."

Briar giggles and I turn, see that even though her cheeks are still pink, her eyes a little damp (and River's are the same), she's smiling.

So is River.

Something unknots in my chest.

I thought I had to be perfect, thought if I just did things exactly the way he preferred then he'd keep his fists to himself...

Keep his fists to himself.

Christ.

I was going to find this ex of hers and make his life miserable.

My gaze drifts to Thorn and I see that same resolve in his expression.

Good.

Double the misery for that asshole.

"You know what?" River says, not looking at me—or Thorn. "Let's leave the bread for tomorrow. I think I have some scalloped potatoes in the freezer that will go perfectly with the chicken." She turns and starts bustling around the kitchen, pots and pans clanging, the fridge and freezer opening and closing.

Thorn shifts uncomfortably. "Maybe I should—"

"Meow. Meow. *Meow!*"

I grin. "I think someone wants a little time with you."

"But—"

"Meow!"

I pat him on the shoulder, pick up the bag of toys and bring it to the couch. Then I cross over to Briar. "You okay?"

A nod.

But her face tells me she's not okay. Not yet. Though... maybe she's getting there.

The past is still heavy. What I did still hangs between us, for all that she says she understands. The threat continues to loom.

And...well, I haven't been giving her space.

Or maybe I have—in my own way.

Going into the office when I don't need to so she has time to settle and a safe place to stay and River and Chrissy, Marie and Rory dropping by on the regular.

And kittens.

Though, I can't reasonably take credit for that part.

Still, I haven't tried to sweet-talk my way into her—*my*—bed. No intense kisses or stroking her gorgeous, naked skin. Just spending time together and with good people and carrying her into the bedroom every night after she falls asleep on my shoulder, dying a little inside when I tuck her beneath the covers and have to say goodnight.

And sleep down the hall.

Alone.

So maybe there's been *some* space.

Space to find herself again. To understand she's safe. To decide if she'll be able to trust me.

Because Pascal was right about one thing—she needs time to heal.

Even if it kills me.

"I'm good," she murmurs.

I touch her cheek. "Yeah?"

Her mouth hitches up. "If not *good* then I'm at least getting there." She shifts closer as Thorn cradles the kitten, walks into the kitchen, his expression unreadable as he watches River throw dinner together. "You?"

"Good. Though, I'm going to miss little Violet."

She sighs. "I know. It's not like taking care of them was planned, but it's been a nice distraction from everything else going on."

The chaos of a half-dozen kittens is certainly that.

"I'm sure Chrissy didn't create this setup"—I wave a hand at the plethora of cat paraphernalia—"without the intention of foisting more kittens on us."

Briar's mouth quirks, but she doesn't argue the *us*.

Which has me wanting to fist pump like an idiot.

"I think the kittens are just the gateway drug," she says. "If Rory has her way, we'll be watching dogs next."

We'll.

My heart leaps in my chest even though I keep it cool on the outside by just shrugging. "I'd be down with a dog or two."

"In your apartment?" She swivels, as though assessing the space. "It's plenty big, I guess, and the patio could work with one of those fake grass potty things. Taking them down in the elevator for walks and stuff would be annoying, though."

"We could wait until we're back at our house."

She stills, her eyes coming to mine. "*Our* house?"

I nod. "Living here means the commute is easy, so I usually stay a couple days a week. But when we're not trying to keep you out of the crosshairs of a criminal organization, I spend most of my time on the estate." Something obvious occurs to me. "Are you uncomfortable being there, considering all that happened between us?"

It would be understandable.

Before everything went wrong, we were building a life in that house, and even if it's the property I inherited from my family, there's no reason we couldn't have a fresh start somewhere new, somewhere without baggage or history.

"No," she says after a moment. "I..." A breath. "I really like your house—"

"*Our* house."

She starts to shake her head.

"I haven't changed a thing, baby."

"What?"

"You made it into a home. I hadn't had that..."

"Since your mom died."

I nod.

She moves closer, wraps me in her arms.

Hugging me. Touching me.

Not the other way around.

Something unlocks in my chest as she smooths her hands up and down my back. "It's been a long time," I say on a shrug. "And I barely remember her anyway."

"Doesn't mean it hurts any less."

Especially when my dad was determined to erase her...and erase any part of her softness that remained in my life.

Boarding school was almost a relief.

Hell, it was probably the only reason I didn't end up sucked into the shit he was involved in.

I want to stay like this forever, holding Briar as she holds me right back, but I'm distinctly aware of River's harried voice, the slams and bangs from the kitchen.

The soft "Meows" from below.

Pulling back, I bend and snag Tulip and Buttercup, cuddling them close. They nuzzle at my face and Tulip wraps her little paws around me in her version of a kitty hug.

I don't think Thorn is the only one who's been claimed.

But I don't mind in the least.

"Should we rescue Thorn from River?" Briar stage whispers as she steals Buttercup from me. "Or is it the other way around?"

I look up, realize what I missed before—namely the look on Thorn's face.

Hmm.

"I'm not sure."

She giggles and we both start walking.

"Brooks?" she says.

"Yeah, baby?"

"We do have to change *one* thing before we go back to our house."

Our house.

The words nearly send me to my knees with relief, but I manage to ask in a semi-reasonable tone, "What's that?"

Her eyes come to mine and the sparkle of humor in them has my heart rolling over in my chest.

Because it's a glimpse of the Briar of old.

"The sensor on that window in your office."

THIRTY-SIX

BRIAR

I WATCH as River sets the platter on the counter.

That she pauses to do even that seems like a freaking miracle, considering her flurry of movements over the last twenty minutes.

But dinner is cooked.

The house is spotless...or as spotless as it can be with a litter of kittens who have an influx of toys, supplemented all the more by Thorn's additions.

"Well," she says, brushing her hands on her pants. "I'll just head out."

"Why don't you stay and eat with us?" I ask.

"Thanks for the offer, sweetheart, but I'd better be getting home."

My eyes flick to Thorn.

He's still standing in the kitchen, still holding Violet, who's curled up against his chest.

But he doesn't say anything as River bustles toward the

front door, grabbing her coat and purse and disappearing through the front door.

He does, however, kiss the top of Violet's head before setting the kitty down on her feet and following River into the hall.

Without another word.

I turn to Brooks, lift my brows.

He just shrugs. "I guess it's dinner only for the two of us?"

Grinning, I grab some plates and utensils and we make short work of dishing up the delicious food that River made, despite my best efforts to drop it on the floor.

It's quiet, almost strange, and I realize I've gotten used to the revolving door of Brooks's friends in the apartment—the rapid-fire conversations, the laughter and stories, Pascal materializing from the shadows with updates about his efforts to track down the Lyon family and whoever they're working with.

Updates that have brought less than the desired result.

Namely because I'd love for some fictional god to appear and smite them off the face of the Earth, never to bother me or Brooks or any of us ever again.

And also because...I need to get the hell out of this apartment.

I'm not going to do anything to jeopardize what everyone's working toward, not going to put myself in danger.

But I am going a little insane just living here, waiting for the other shoe to drop.

Now that I'm not worried about where my next meal is coming from or whether I'll be able to afford my apartment, I need a purpose.

I want to do normal things—go to the grocery store, walk through the park, have dinner in a restaurant. And I want to live without worrying about when the next letter will show up, if it'll slip through the precautions that Pascal and his team have put in place, what will happen to Brooks if I don't do what they want.

"Did Pascal find anything?" Thorn had discovered a targeted email campaign at his company and Pascal had put his team on trying to track down where they'd originated from.

"Only that they were sent from France."

Where Jean-Michel, Brooks, Jace and Thorn all have homes and business ties.

Where the Lyon family has the same.

It seems freaking obvious, but they're good at what they do, great at covering their tracks.

"It's the USB," I say.

He takes the two plates, sets them on the pair of placemats River laid out. "Baby, you need to stop beating yourself up about that. Chrissy knows and Pascal says it was clunky and wouldn't have worked as you were instructed anyway."

"That's something else that bugs me."

He snags a bottle of wine from the fridge, two glasses from the cabinet. "Why?"

"Because every other time I did a job for them, it was..." I trail off because I don't really know what to say. Not effective, necessarily. Things went wrong and I made plenty of mistakes throughout those years on my own. Mistakes I paid for—physically and otherwise. Over time I had to learn to do reconnaissance, however effective it was. I already knew how to blend in, that part was easy since I spent my childhood trying to hide in plain sight, not wanting to face the wrath of my grandfather.

So I suppose, even though there were challenges, it always felt more put together.

I had more time. It was thought out.

I wasn't breaking into my ex's home with three days' notice, infiltrating a winery event mere days after that.

And then there's the fact that the USB wouldn't have worked like I was told it would.

I shake my head because that matters.

And it doesn't.

"That's not the drive I'm talking about." I take a breath. "I mean the one from your safe."

His face gentles. "There was nothing on there that's important, baby. Yes, I did what I thought was right to keep you safe over the last five years—and yeah, some of it definitely bordered on illegal and wrong—"

He'd already told me about paying the blackmail, about signing over the business and houses to the Lyons.

"—but the companies I kept are clear of anything unlawful," he says. "And all of that happened after my father died, so he wouldn't have been able to document it, even if he wanted to."

"I get that it wouldn't hurt you today—or not much, anyway." I nibble at the corner of my mouth. "But it could have hurt your father when he was alive...and I guess I'm thinking that if *that's* true, it also could have hurt anyone else who was involved in his businesses at that time—especially the bad ones you distanced yourself from."

I pause, waiting for him to say something.

But he just stares at me, his eyes gone wide.

Then he bursts to his feet.

"Time to call Pascal?" I ask.

He nods, pulls out his phone.

And makes the call.

———

I FINISH PACKING up the leftovers, make sure the kitties are settled in for the night, then glance down the hall.

Pascal is in Brooks's office and has been there a while.

And maybe I should let them continue to talk. I don't know all that was on the drive. I don't have it any longer. And truly, I don't even know if it *is* important—though, I have to presume it is considering that the powers that be went through the trouble of having me steal it.

Still, I may be completely off base.

But I don't think so.

And I don't want Brooks to have to deal with this alone.

Space and time. Patience and kindness. And love, so much love it burned through my veins like lava when he left, bubbled like champagne during our happy moments, and now flows like a raging river, swollen from the snowmelt as I walk down the hall.

Love that never faded. Need that never waned. Peace that I can only find with him by my side.

I approach the door, lifting my hand to knock.

But it's slightly ajar, their voices drifting out into the hall.

And what I hear Pascal say is a bucket of icy water dumped over my head.

"I still think you're making a mistake by not leaving."

But what Brooks says in return is worse.

"Maybe you're right."

THIRTY-SEVEN

BROOKS

"I STILL THINK you're making a mistake by not leaving."

"Maybe you're right," I say and sigh. "Maybe I shouldn't be here. Maybe I should walk away." I hold his stare. "But I'm not going to."

He opens his mouth.

"And don't say that I did before. I'm not going to rehash this shit but we both did what we thought was best and yes, it was the biggest fucking mistake of my life, but I'm not going to keep apologizing for it, keep fucking up my present, my future—"

"Good."

Only, it's not Pascal saying that.

It's Briar.

Fuck, how much had she overheard?

"Raindrop," I rasp.

She moves over to me, eyes sad, and my heart sinks. "I don't know how much you heard—"

"I'm sorry," she says.

I blink. "You have nothing to apologize for."

She shakes her head. "You explained. I told you I under-stand—and I *do*. But I threw it back in your face, didn't make it clear that I'm here too. That I'm not going *anywhere*. So yeah," she says. "I do have to apologize. I'm sorry." She cups my face in her hands. "Because if it meant keeping you safe, I would have done *anything*, even if that meant breaking your heart, even if that meant you hated me."

Movement catches my eye and I glance over her shoulder, see Pascal standing in the doorway.

He winks at me and then disappears—fucking *disappears*.

Or maybe it's that I'm more worried about the woman in my arms.

"I won't bring it up again, I promise," she says.

"It's going to take time for you to trust in me, in us," I remind her. "I get that. But seriously, baby, you don't need to apologize."

She shakes her head, clearly not agreeing with me. "You're right, you know. I never stopped loving you."

"Briar."

"And I know that we can't go back," she murmurs as I draw her close, inhaling the scent of her, feeling the softness of her body. "But I want to move forward together." She nibbles at her bottom lip. "That is...if you still want that."

My heart leaps.

Then immediately sinks.

"Why would you think I don't want that?"

"I—" Her cheeks go pink. "Well, I mean, you haven't exactly—"

"I haven't...what?"

"You haven't tried to..." Those cheeks go even pinker. "You know..."

"No"—I draw her closer—"I *don't* know."

That makes her scowl and swat me lightly on her chest. "Don't tease."

"I like teasing you," I murmur, skating my hand down her spine. "And I think you like it when I tease you too."

Her hands come back to my face and she cups my cheeks again, stares deeply into my eyes.

"What?" I ask.

"Tell me," she orders.

I almost ask her what it is she wants me to say. But, deep down, I know. "I was trying to give you space."

She smiles softly. "Pascal?"

"Yes." I sigh. "And no."

"You did need space, baby. And a place to be safe, plus time to not be strictly in survival mode. But I wasn't going to leave you alone while that happened."

Her eyes are damp as she whispers, "I know."

"And *I* know that a couple of therapy appointments, some time with good people, and consistent meals can't fix everything."

"Don't forget the kittens," she adds lightly.

"Who's the one teasing now?" I draw my finger down her nose, tap lightly. "I *was* pushing. Pascal wasn't right about me leaving, but he was right about that. So, I figured I could give you space to settle and still be here. Though..." I think of the smirk on my friend's face, the wink he gave me before he left.

"What?"

"I wonder if he knew it would make me double down so I didn't act like an idiot while we were figuring this shit out."

She pauses, considers that. Then her lips curve. "I wouldn't put it past him. He seems to consider all the angles while the rest of us are just struggling to keep up."

I don't disagree with her. But—

"What do you mean?"

"He knew I needed to forgive myself." She exhales and I brace, knowing with one glimpse of her eyes that I'm not going to like what she says next. "For not being enough."

I frown.

"My parents didn't love me. My grandpa didn't either. And then..."

She doesn't finish.

But she doesn't have to.

"Then I left," I say, the truth tearing through me. "*I didn't love you enough.*"

"Brooks, I didn't mean—"

I settle my forehead on hers. "I know."

"And I'm..." Her throat works. "Well, the truth is that I'm still working through all of that. I know logically it wasn't really about me—"

"But that doesn't mean the feelings have gone away either. I get that. Hell, this stuff with the USB, the things my dad did in the past, and how it all might be connected to everything we've gone through—" I tuck her hair behind her ear. "It's not like I can just pack that all away and pretend it won't come back up again, pretend it doesn't fuck with my head."

"Exactly," she whispers.

"Want to know the good thing?"

A nod.

"We have time. We don't have to rush. We can just be us as we sort our heads and hearts out."

She leans against me, arms around my waist, expression soft, eyes warm. "As long as we do it together."

God, this woman *undoes* me.

So, I say the only thing I can,

"As you wish."

I tug the covers over Briar, lean down and press my lips to her forehead.

She smells faintly of popcorn and the kittens have made a mess of her braid.

But she's still the most beautiful woman I've ever seen.

Hair turned silver in the moonlight, her face serene in a way that heals the jagged wound inside me.

We switched to watching a show that Chrissy recommended—one I only capitulated to because Briar seemed so excited to have something to discuss with the rest of the girls.

It's a cheesy reality drama, but I can't lie...there was a dash of romance that I enjoyed.

Damn woman.

Hooking me on something the guys will give me shit about.

But fuck, I'm looking forward to that.

TV shows and Jace giving me a hard time. Briar smiling as she curls up next to me...and never failing to fall asleep cuddled close, her head under my chin, her steady breaths on my throat.

Leaving the rest of the popcorn for me.

I really like that part.

Almost as much as I like the feel of her in my arms.

Grinning, I fuss with the blankets and straighten, knowing I need to let her sleep, but when I go to turn away, her hand finds mine.

"Stay?" she asks, lids half-mast, her eyes drowsy.

"As you wish."

Who's the cheesy one now?

But I can't help it.

I love this woman to distraction.

Her lips curve and I climb under the blankets, slipping my arms around her, and for the first time in five years, I fall asleep knowing that everything is going to be okay.

THIRTY-EIGHT

BRIAR

I WAKE SLOWLY but not for a second do I wonder where I am.

I'm in Brooks's bed.

In his arms.

His breathing is steady and even but I know he's awake.

He nuzzles at my hair, presses a kiss to my nape. "You sleep okay?"

Did I sleep okay?

"I feel..."

He smooths his hand down my back, waits patiently for me to get my brain together—because of course he does.

"Good," I finally finish, when it's not the right word, can't begin to encompass what I'm feeling.

Because it's like all the pieces are coming together.

He chuckles and I roll over in his arms.

"Not the most effusive word choice, I know," I say, stroking my fingers through the stubble. "It's just like...this is right and easy." His eyes hold mine. "It's like I'm whole again, you know?"

The past isn't gone. The threat still looms.

But somehow, for the first time maybe ever, I know it's all going to be okay.

"Yeah, baby. I know *exactly* what you mean." He sighs and draws me closer. "You know the only good thing about us being apart?"

"What's that?"

"I know how fucking lucky I am to have you back and I will never, *ever* take it for granted."

My eyes burn as that flows over me—how much I can see he feels it, how much I feel the same.

But I don't want to go back to us apologizing to each other.

We've done that.

And I meant what I said about moving forward.

So I blink back the tears and snuggle closer. "I think there's another thing you're forgetting about."

"There is?"

"Did you or did you not make it clear to Jace that he should get over himself and keep Marie forever?"

He stills then his chuckle ruffles through my hair. "There may have been just a modicum of ass-kicking."

I giggle. "Ass kicking? Or his head being removed from said ass?"

Another chuckle. "Either. Both."

"I thought so." I shift a little closer then barely hold back a gasp when he hitches my leg over his hip, draws me flush against him. "Marie seems to think you played a bit more than matchmaker."

"Eh"—his hand slides down my back—"I think Jean-Michel had as much of a hand in it as I did."

"Why doesn't that surprise me?"

"It does seem like he manages to be everywhere—or at least has sources everywhere."

It does seem to be that way. Although...

"Maybe it's really Pascal who's behind it all."

A laugh. "Probably. The man *does* disappear into shadows."

"How does he do that?"

"No clue." Brooks nuzzles at my jaw. "Though, you're the one who snuck into our supposedly secure house without being seen. I think you might have the melting into shadows thing down pat."

"I had inside information from living there."

"Maybe." A beat. "Or maybe you're just damned impressive."

I feel my cheeks get hot, but before I can demure, can point out that I just did what I had to, same as him, he kisses me.

It's not the kiss I expect.

Instead of being hot and wet and deep—I mean, my leg is wrapped around him, the hard length of his erection pressing into me—it's gentle and sweet, so damned sweet it has my eyes prickling with tears again.

I slide my hands into his hair, lips parting, tongue slipping into his mouth. "More," I whisper.

He goes still. "We don't have to rush, baby. We can take our—"

"More," I demand against his lips, fingers tightening in his hair.

He groans and suddenly, I'm on my back, his hard body pressed into mine, his eyes molten, and his body—

"Oh!" I gasp when he rocks his erection against me.

His mouth hitches up. Then he's kissing me again, his hand slipping under my tank top, skating up along my side. I can feel him trying to throttle his need, to stay in control.

But I don't want him in control.

I just want Brooks.

I wrap my legs around his waist and arch my back, pressing my breast into his hand when it comes close.

He hisses out a breath then molds my flesh with his fingers, brushes his thumb over my nipple. Then his mouth is descending over mine and our tongues are tangling.

And this kiss is very much *not* nice.

It's deep and wet, hot and slick, and it sends my thoughts scattering and my body into overdrive.

I drag my nails over his back, clutching at the material of his shirt and yanking it up. He lurches back, rips it over his head, tossing it to the side.

"You are so fucking beautiful," I murmur then smile when a hint of red coats his cheeks. But I only get to see that for a second before his hands are dragging my tank top up.

He groans again. "You're the beautiful one."

Then his mouth is coming to mine and we're kissing and kissing and *kissing*, our bodies rocking together as though they remember the precise rhythm that drives us both insane. Fingers trail over my skin, roll my nipples, slip between my legs and stroke—

"Oh God!" I cry, breaking the kiss, my head dropping back when he presses his palm to my clit, when he circles and presses and pinches. "Oh, my fucking *God!*"

His lips trail down my throat, moving steadily toward my breasts.

He takes a nipple in his mouth, making me cry out again as waves of pleasure flow through my body.

"So fucking wet," he groans, stroking through the slick folds of my labia, circling my entrance. "I want you so fucking much."

"Then take me," I pant. "Now, Brooks."

His smile makes me shiver.

"Later," he murmurs.

Then he's kissing his way down my body, tossing my legs over his shoulders, and—

Licking and sucking, stroking and biting. Devouring me with his mouth, sending me skittering to the edge of release in just a few minutes. But I don't want to go without him. This time, this moment I want to share with him.

"Brooks," I say, winding my fingers into his hair and tugging. "Not without you."

He nips at the inside of my thigh and I have to clench my teeth together, have to tighten every muscle in my body to keep from flying over the edge. "Baby, I haven't been with anyone in five years. I'm only going to last like ten seconds. Let me make you feel good first."

"You haven't—?"

Those eyes come to mine as he presses a finger into me. "No."

"I—"

"I don't care if you have," he interjects before I can finish.

I tug at his hair before he can distract me again. "It's only ever been you," I say. "I need you to know that."

His shoulders lift and drop on a breath. "Baby—"

"And I need you now. I need us to do this together."

"Raindrop," he rasps and I don't miss the dampness in his eyes as he comes back over me. His mouth finds mine and I can taste myself on his lips, his tongue. But I don't mind. In fact, I like it, like how it's another example of the two of us coming together.

Then he's kneeling between my legs, the hard jut of his erection nudging at my entrance.

"Ready?" he rasps.

I touch his cheek. "Now, honey."

His eyes close and then he's sliding into me, stretching me in the best possible way.

He shudders, and I can't help but break the kiss, my head dropping back, my legs tightening around him.

A groan vibrates through him when he bottoms out and I hold still for a second, just sitting in the way he's possessing me so completely.

"Okay?" he grits out, the question barely discernible.

I nod, demand, "More."

He takes me at my word—pulling back, thrusting in—and it takes all of two seconds for it to feel like someone has set me on fire. I was already close, already hovering on the edge of an orgasm, but the way he moves has my control fracturing.

I dig my nails into his back, match his strokes.

They're hurried and hard, hitting a spot deep inside me that drives me insane.

"Brooks!" I cry, feeling it coming, knowing it's going to be big.

Big.

So big it may incinerate me.

But that's okay.

Because he's right there with me.

"Come for me, baby," he groans, sweat glistening on his forehead. "*Now,* Raindrop. I need you to come for me."

I lift my hips, meeting those hard thrusts, grinding my clit against him.

And it's right there.

And, oh fuck, it's intense, so big it drags me under, that pleasure exploding through me.

He calls my name, his strokes going wild, and he absolutely pounds into me as I come and come and *come.*

I collapse back to the mattress, limbs numb, vision hazy— and completely obliterated by the orgasm he just gave me.

But even as I float through that cloud of pleasure, I'm aware of Brooks holding me, touching me...

Loving me.

And I'm determined to love him right back.

Forever.

THIRTY-NINE

BROOKS

I LOOK at the report and sigh. "What do you think?"

Pascal looks as frustrated as I feel. "I *think* I wish we had more, but we're not getting anywhere."

Damn.

He's not wrong—as fucking much as that pisses me off.

It's been almost two months since I brought Briar back to my apartment and we're not getting anywhere with the investigation. Every time we tease a lead loose, think we've found the location of the people who were hurting Briar, who were fucking with our businesses, it doesn't pan out. Hell, I'd even take a criminal connection to the Lyon family, something concrete and not just rumor or general knowledge.

I'm not above using blackmail to keep Briar safe.

But we don't even have that.

Sighing, I lean back in my chair, ask, "Next steps?"

"The way I see it, you have two options: pull back the security measures—or at least give the appearance of doing so—and see if we can get these fuckers to bite."

"Draw them out and take them down," I say.

He nods. "I don't think they're dumb enough to fall for that, though."

I agree. "What's the other option?"

"You're not going to like it."

"Probably not but tell me anyway."

"You make it look like Briar's on her own again, and when they take advantage of that *then* we take them down."

"I'm not using Briar as bait," I snap.

"You guys can't continue living like this—Briar cooped up in your apartment, you limiting your own movements to your office and the couple of places we know are safe." His hands clench into fists. "As much as it pains me, this investigation could go on for months, for fucking *years*. So you need to either be prepared for that, or you need to give them a push and hope they make a mistake."

"Putting her at risk isn't acceptable."

He sighs.

I scowl. "Weren't you the one who was saying we should keep her far away from this shit?"

"Yes. But she's had some time to heal now. She's stronger, and that strength won't continue to grow if she's stuck living in the shadows."

"What?" I mutter. "You're a philosopher now?"

He rolls his eyes. "She's a survivor and I want what's best for her."

"Well, I don't think *what's best for her* is swinging her ass out there."

"Just talk to her, see what she thinks. Trust her enough with the reality."

I scowl.

Mostly because I know I need to do exactly that. "Fine," I mutter. "As long as you promise to keep digging."

He just gives me an affronted look and stands, but before he can disappear into the shadows, my cell rings.

My eyes flick to the screen, see it's Briar, and I swipe. "Hi, baby."

"Is River sick?"

"No." I frown. "River's not sick."

Pascal had been turning for the door, but my statement has him stopping.

He moves back over to me, gestures at my phone.

"I'm putting you on speaker, okay? Pascal's here."

"Oh, uh, sure."

I jab at the button. "You there?"

"Yes." Her voice is laced with worry. "I'm here, but River hasn't shown up yet. I know she kind of makes her own hours, but we planned on trying out a couple of new recipes today and she mentioned being here by now."

"Is there anything else you see that's out of the ordinary?" Pascal asks.

She pauses, breath coming through the speakers. "No, I don't think so. Buttercup and Tulip are sleeping together on their bed and the front door is locked. The internet is working and the phone too, obviously." Another sigh. "It's all just... normal."

"Except, there's no River."

"Yeah."

There's a knock at my office door and we both look up, see Thorn pushing through, his scowl even fiercer than normal. "You need to see this," he snaps, tossing down an envelope on my desk that has my heart convulsing.

The picture—

"Fuck," Pascal hisses.

"What?" Briar asks through the phone, voice frantic.

Thorn's gaze comes to mine and I have to force the words out through clenched teeth.

"They have River."

FORTY

BRIAR

I PACE THROUGH THE APARTMENT, my heart pounding, worry gnawing at every inch of my body.

They have River.

They have her.

Fists and sharp words, guns and fear filling every cell of my body. No freedom. Forced to do what they want. And feeling so fucking hopeless.

"Dammit," I whisper, swiping at my cheeks as my tears spill over.

Freaking out isn't going to help, I know that.

I need to be calm. Need to let Pascal do his thing.

But what if his *thing* yields the same results of the last few months?

Nothing.

I know exactly how dangerous the Lyons are.

They haven't been able to get me here in Brooks's apartment, but only because I've stayed on the top floor, living like a princess locked away in a tower, security monitoring each and every person accessing the building.

Groceries delivered.

Foster kittens and their gear too—though Buttercup and Tulip are officially ours now.

Friends coming here, and only here.

Safety. Companionship. Food. Connection.

I've had everything I need, even *if* I've been going more than a bit stir crazy.

Still, I've started filling out my life—signing up for several online classes, helping Chrissy and Rory with some administration work for their charities, trying and failing at several new hobbies.

Turns out I'm hopeless when it comes to quilting.

And crocheting. And embroidery.

Maybe I'll try out scrapbooking next.

After we get my friend back.

My phone buzzes and my heart lurches, thinking it might be *them*.

But it's just Brooks.

I swipe. "You find her?"

The pause before he replies tells me enough. No, they haven't found her.

"Never mind," I murmur. "What do you need?"

Another pause before his tone goes deliberately gentle. "Are you okay to look at a photograph?" he asks. My brows drag together but before I can say *of course*, he adds, "River's in it, Raindrop. And it's not going to be easy to look at."

I inhale.

Fuck. *Fuck.*

Then I shove that all down. "Send me the picture."

"You sure?"

"Yes." I take a breath. "Let me help."

A blip of quiet. "Okay, baby. Hang on, I'm sending it over."

There's a rustling, the whoosh of the text being sent, and a moment later, my cell buzzes. I put him on speaker, bring up the message, and the image slams into me, nearly sending me to my knees. I inhale sharply, vision going black at the edges.

"Briar?" Brooks's voice is worried, like he's called my name more than once.

"I'm okay," I whisper. "They took me there. When I..." Memories cascade through my brain and I have to breathe through them. "When I wouldn't do what they wanted, that's where they would hurt me."

Someone curses and before I can place the voice, there's a crash that has me jumping.

"Brooks?" I ask.

"It's okay," he says. "Thorn is here, he's the one who got the letter, and"—he hesitates—"and he's not taking it well."

"Oh."

"Can you tell us where the location is?" Pascal asks.

I close my eyes, shake my head. Then realize they can't see me through the phone. "No," I say. "They always took me in the middle of the night and blindfolded me during the drive."

"So it was within driving distance?" he asks.

"Yes," I say, forcing myself to think beyond the fear and painful memories, trying to ferret out any details that might help them. "It wasn't a long drive. Maybe an hour and—" I stop, think, *breathe*. "It was definitely near the ocean. I could smell the salt in the air, hear the crash of the waves when they brought me inside."

"And what did *inside* look like?"

I tell them about the bodies bumping into mine as they led me down a narrow staircase, the echo of voices when I was brought into a large open room. A warehouse that would sometimes be empty, sometimes full of boxes on pallets.

"I didn't get good glimpses of their faces," I say. "It was dark and cold and I was scared. But the floor..." I tug at the memory. "There was a logo on the floor." Yellow peeling paint, the black outlines of letters forming—

"It was a French name. Jardeaux? Jarnac? Jar—"

"—din?" I hear Thorn ask.

"Yes, that's it."

"Jardin Logistics," Thorn says. "They do international fulfillment for my company."

Quiet falls.

"We need to move on this quickly," Brooks says, and though I have the feeling he's not talking to me, I tell them, "Go. I'll text if I think of anything else that might be helpful."

"Thanks, Raindrop," Brooks murmurs.

"Just find her."

"We will," he promises.

I hang up, know they're going to do their best to keep that promise.

But as the hours pass and no word comes, the knot in my stomach grows.

Because I know exactly how dangerous these people can be.

———

My phone rings and I jerk, dislodging Tulip and Buttercup.

Normally, their meows of protests would be adorable, making me smile as I cuddled them close again.

But I'm too focused on muting the movie I'm not watching and answering the call.

"Brooks?"

"We found her," he says. "She's okay and Pascal's team detained the men who were holding her."

Relief has me melting back into the couch cushions. "Thank God. Is she okay?"

"A little banged up, but otherwise she's all right. I'm still at the office since Pascal had to pull guys from here and the apartment to join in on the operation, but he's going to swing by and pick me up once they're close. The rest of the team is heading directly back to you with River. They should be there in a little under an hour."

"What does she need?"

"I'm not entirely sure, Raindrop," he murmurs. "But I suspect a safe space to land and time to heal."

"We can give her that."

"Yes, we can."

There are voices in the background. "I need to go, baby. I'll be there soon and we'll figure everything out."

We exchange "I love you"s and goodbyes and hang up.

I sit in my relief for a second before nervous energy ripples through me and I jump to my feet. I'll make her something.

Cookies or banana bread or—

No, just bread.

River's sourdough starter is in the fridge.

I'll make her that quick bread she likes.

Bustling into the kitchen, I start gathering ingredients—flour and the starter, eggs and baking soda and salt. I decide to get crazy and shred some cheddar cheese, chop a jalapeño.

Just as I'm pouring the batter into the pan, the doorbell rings.

I glance at the clock over the stove.

That was fast.

Hurrying to the door, I don't really process that Pascal's crew all have codes to the front door, that they wouldn't have knocked and waited for me to answer, especially with River in tow.

A cursory knock before coming in?
Yeah.
Standing on the other side until I open the wooden panel?
No.
But that thought doesn't cross my mind—
Not until I twist the knob, open the door, and...
See the woman pointing a gun at me.
The Lyons have found me again.

FORTY-ONE

BRIAR

"YOU DON'T HAVE to do this," I say as Angela herds me back, closing the door behind her.

The deadbolt sliding shut is gunshot—no pun intended—loud in the quiet apartment.

She's tall and slender, her blonde hair pulled back into a neat chignon, and the sunglasses on her face don't hide the bruising around her black eye. She moves carefully, as though she's protecting her ribs, but her grip on the gun is steady.

"I don't have much time," she says. "So I need you to sit down, shut up, and listen to me."

Maybe I could overpower her, especially considering she's hurt.

But I've seen this woman endure things that would break me, so I know that even though she appears weak, she's anything but.

"Okay," I say calmly, not loving the gun pointed in my direction, but doing my best to ignore it.

"Is there anyone else in the apartment?" she asks.

I shake my head. "Just the cats."

She doesn't move, but I have the feeling that her gaze is flicking around the room, assessing if I'm telling the truth.

Then she seems to decide that I am.

"Sit." She gestures to the barstool with her gun.

I sit and the silence stretches as we just look at each other.

Then she walks over to me, slides her hand into her pocket. "Here," she mutters. "Use this. It'll keep you and the other girl safe."

"I don't understand."

A sigh as she sets the envelope on the counter. "I'm supposed to use the distraction they created by taking her to eliminate the problem you present."

Fear skitters up my spine.

"But I've been doing a lot of things I shouldn't these last few months. That—" A nod to the envelope. "That will damage them enough they'll need to close ranks and regroup."

"How long until they come after me and Brooks and my friends again?"

"They'll decide it's not worth the trouble. There are plenty of easier targets with fewer resources now that the personal side has been settled."

"I don't understand."

"I don't expect you to," she says. "But I'm doing what I can —I made it so Brooks is back in your life and Chrissy's baby will be safe—" She breaks off.

My heart starts pounding. "What does Chrissy have to do with me?"

Something passes over her face and I suck in a breath.

"Wait," I whisper, the information clicking into place. "You're *that* Angela?"

"I don't know what you're talking about."

"You're Angela Rosseau? Jean-Michel's ex, Chrissy's mom —" I shake my head. "But you're crazy."

She jerks and I clamp my mouth closed.

Probably shouldn't call the woman pointing a gun at me crazy.

"Sorry," I whisper.

But she doesn't squeeze the trigger and prove that point. Instead, she laughs softly. "Yeah, Briar. I'm definitely crazy."

"Meow."

"Buttercup," I begin. "She—"

But Angela just tucks the gun into the waistband of her jeans, crouches down and scratches Buttercup—then Tulip, when she comes over—behind their ears.

"How did you make sure Brooks was back in my life?"

Her gaze comes to mine and I wish I could see through the dark lenses of her glasses. "He's one of the good ones." A sigh as she straightens. "There aren't too many of those around. I needed to make it right—for both of you."

"I'm just—"

"One of the good ones too," she says softly.

"I don't understand."

"I know." Another nod to the envelope. "Use it," she says. "No matter how much you don't want to."

She turns toward the door and I find myself blurting, "They can help you—Pascal and Brooks."

Still. God, she's so freaking *still*.

Then she pushes her glasses to the top of her head and our gazes collide.

Fuck, that bruise around her eye is awful.

"No one can help me," she murmurs.

"I—"

"Bermuda," she says.

"What?"

"That's when I knew you were one of the good ones."

I suck in another breath, remember the little girl I'd returned to her parents...and the beating I received for not following through with my orders to get her onto the boat that would have taken her who knew where for who knew what.

Okay, I knew what would happen to her.

And I couldn't let that happen.

"Oh, my God," I whisper. "That's why you—"

Angela had come with me on the next few missions and after that the tasks I was assigned had changed. No more close calls with pervy men they needed blackmail material for. No more kids or women.

There's a knock and a whir, the lock disengaging.

Her head whips toward the door as it slams into the deadbolt and she moves faster than I thought possible, grabbing a chair and jamming it under the handle.

Yeah, I so wouldn't have been able to disarm her.

The door pulls back then slams open again, meeting the resistance of the deadbolt—and now the chair.

"Briar!" I hear Brooks shout from the other side.

"I'm okay!" I call and stand up.

But freeze, when the gun points my way again.

"Stay there," she says quietly as the door starts reverberating, Brooks trying to break through. I freeze, sit back down, and she turns for the hall as the noise becomes almost deafening.

That door isn't going to hold much longer.

"Angela!" I call.

Her eyes come to mine.

"How did you know Brooks and I would work it out?"

A pregnant pause.

"True love," she says just before the chair splinters, the deadbolt gives way, and Brooks shoves his way through the opening, Pascal's team pushing through behind him.

He rushes over to me.

They spot her and give chase—

But she's already sprinting down the hall, disappearing into the bedroom.

And by the time they make it through that locked door, then through the one into the bathroom, she's given Pascal a run for his money and disappeared.

Leaving nothing but a series of broken doors, an open skylight, and...

Our salvation on the counter.

FORTY-TWO

BROOKS

"OH FUCK," I whisper, hauling Briar against my chest and holding her tight. "Oh fuck."

"I'm okay," she whispers back.

There's chaos all around us—Pascal and his team bustling around the apartment, clearing every room, searching for any surveillance equipment that may have been left behind.

Angela Rosseau.

With a fucking gun.

Angela. I should have registered the name when Briar mentioned it months ago, should have realized it was Jean-Michel's ex and Chrissy's mother behind all this shit...or at least mixed up in it.

But I had been far more focused on all Briar went through and bridging the gulf between us.

And now Angela had pointed a gun at the woman I loved.

"She wasn't going to hurt me," Briar says when I just haul

her closer and try to breathe through the panic still coursing through my body.

The door is fucked and we'll have to find somewhere else to stay for tonight.

"I know you want to believe that, but she's insane—Attie was shot and Chrissy was almost kidnapped and River *was* taken, and that was all because of her. And she pulled a fucking gun on you, baby."

Briar sighs and snuggles closer. "I know."

I wrap my arms tighter, ignoring the pain radiating down from my shoulder. "I'm sorry."

"It's not your fault," she says. "I was dumb. I was thinking about River and opened the door without checking who was on the other side."

"It's been a scary day."

"But even if I checked, I think…"

"What?"

"I think I probably would have still let her in."

"Briar," I say, releasing her and leaning back enough to see her face.

Her eyes are earnest and the set of her jaw warns me to brace. "I know what she put Jean-Michel, Chrissy, and Attie through and I hate that they had to deal with it. I also know the people she keeps company with and how bad they are." Her hand finds mine and squeezes. "But I also witnessed the violence she endured, saw the bruise on her face tonight, the way she moved like she was in pain. Whatever her part in all of this is, I don't think it's as straightforward as you all think."

I smooth back her hair, know that she's right.

As much as I hate it.

Angela protected Chrissy when she was almost taken.

Marie is convinced that she stopped her from getting hit by a car.

And Briar...well, what Briar went through was hell, but it does seem like Angela buffered her from some of the worst of it.

"I'm not saying she's all good, but I do know that she helped me, helped *us* find our way back to each other, and"—she snags the envelope off the island, hands it to me—"if this really does have something on it that will protect us, then she's helped us again. So...can we just maybe reserve judgment until we know more?"

"Yeah, Raindrop, we can do that."

Her face goes soft and she shifts closer, wrapping her arms around me. "Thank you," she whispers.

We stay like that—bodies pressed together and standing in the kitchen, waiting for Pascal and his team to search through and clear the rest of the apartment. Aside from passing off the envelope, we're quiet, and I, for one, am just reveling in the fact that everyone is safe.

And that this shit might finally be done.

"Is River still coming here?" she asks as the activity begins to wane.

"No," I say, forcing myself to release her. I stride over to the closet, pulling out a broom and dustpan so I can clean up the remains of the chair. "Thorn took her home."

Her lips twitch.

And for the first time in hours, mine do too.

"It's about time he got his head out of his ass," she says.

"I know," I agree. "Though, almost losing a good woman will do that to a man."

She catches my hand, fingers squeezing mine tight. "Thank you," she whispers.

"For what?"

"For fighting for us. For loving me." A sigh, her head resting against my arm. "For just *being* here."

My heart rolls over in my chest, exposing its vulnerable underbelly.

But I know, without a doubt, this woman will protect it, cherish it, fight for it right back.

"Always," I rasp.

Then, as one, we move to the door and clean up the mess.

The door is fucked, the frame will need to be replaced.

But that's a problem for another day. For tonight—

"Jean-Michel offered to let us stay at his place."

She dumps the contents of the dustpan in the trash and looks up at me. "Is that what you want?"

"As long as we're safe, I don't care where we sleep."

Pretty blue eyes hold mine, and I see the answer in those cerulean depths even before she murmurs, "Then I think it's time for us to go home."

"As you wish."

Her mouth quirks. "God, I love you."

There my heart goes again, so full of love for this woman, of pride and need, of relief that she's safe and hope for the future we're going to build together that I *have* to draw her against me and kiss her with everything I'm feeling.

It takes a while and it isn't the right time or the right place— case in point, the wolf whistles that come from Pascal's men as they move around the space—but I don't care.

Because the woman I love is back in my arms.

And I'm never letting go.

HOURS LATER, we're back in our bedroom, the estate quiet and sprawling around us.

Exhaustion had me dropping into sleep almost the moment my head hit the pillow and my arms were back around her, and it feels like only moments later before she's carefully shifting out of my hold.

I expect to hear her pad to the bathroom.

Instead, I hear the soft shush of the door sliding open and then closed.

Worry has me sitting up, pushing out of bed, moving to that door.

She looks over her shoulder at me as I step onto the patio, mouth curved. "Sorry if I woke you."

I take her in my arms. "You okay?"

"Yeah. I just...it feels strange that this will all finally be over."

For us, that is.

Angela hadn't lied about the envelope containing information that will protect us all.

Now we just have to decide how to use it to move forward.

"I know."

"How do I just live a normal life after all that happened?"

"You don't," I tell her. "You live *your* life."

"No. *Our* life."

I tug lightly at a strand of her hair. "Yeah, Raindrop. Our life."

Her mouth hitches up. "How do you feel about animal rescue?"

"Considering Tulip and Buttercup are sleeping at the foot of our bed, I think it's clear that I'm all in."

"Cats then?"

I shrug. "Or dogs. You know Rory will demand equal representation."

"Or," she says, "I could do something a little different."

"Ferret rescue?"

She giggles and lifts on tiptoe, brushing her mouth over mine. "I was thinking more like...horses." She waves a hand toward the land, quiet and shadowed and hushed. "There's plenty of space—" Her eyes come to mine. "Though, if you don't want the hassle..."

"I think moving the stables to the south side of the property would be perfect, don't you think? There's already open space and it's flat. Plus, it's not too far from the main house."

"Brooks," she whispers.

"This is our future, Raindrop. And you're going to have anything you want."

"What about what *you* want?"

I draw her closer. "I already have it."

There's a sharp crack of noise and the skies seem to open up, rain pouring down, soaking us in an instant.

But we don't rush inside, don't run from the sudden summer rainstorm.

Instead, we both tilt our faces up to the sky...

And we laugh.

And it's the best start to forever I can imagine.

EPILOGUE

BRIAR, ONE MONTH LATER

IT'S RAINING as I step out of the car, the drops plopping onto my head, the dirt below.

Lifting my face up to the sky, knowing it's probably messing up my makeup and not caring, I laugh.

Because...it's raining.

An hour ago there hadn't been a cloud in the sky, not even the barest hint of a storm in the forecast.

And now it's raining.

"Raindrop," I hear, an arm wrapping around my waist, warm lips kissing off the droplets.

Opening my eyes, I grin at Brooks.

"It's raining."

His lips twitch. "Yeah, it is."

I swipe away a drop of rain that's clinging to his eyebrow. "You look devastatingly handsome in that suit."

He grins and it's laced with a wickedness that makes me

want to take his hand and drag him into the back of the car that drove me here.

Too bad the windows aren't tinted.

And that our friends are nearby, gathered in the clearing, hastily opening umbrellas that River is passing out.

River.

My heart squeezes.

She's staying with us, having shown up at the house the week after everything went down...and acting decidedly mum about anything related to Thorn since.

We've done a lot of baking over the last few weeks.

And online classes, trying to figure out our future.

And wedding planning.

And putting together the building blocks for a horse rescue.

But not much talking about why Thorn keeps showing up at the house...and why River keeps refusing to see him.

"I have a surprise for you," Brooks murmurs.

"Is it another car with tinted windows so I can show you how much I love you in that suit?"

His mouth quirks and he smooths back my hair in that gentle way of his. "Damn. That really was a missed opportunity to get you naked, wasn't it?"

Laughter in my chest and bubbling up into the air around us.

"Fuck, you're beautiful."

I wave my hand. "Eh, I had help."

"It's not the makeup or hair, and it's not even the dress. Though"—he settles a hand on my waist, draws me closer—"I fucking *love* the dress, baby."

I shiver, and it's not from the cold.

"What's the surprise?"

He opens his mouth—

"Use the umbrella, dumbass!"

I jerk at Jace's voice, see him get swatted by Marie, who's wearing a gorgeous emerald dress that's the same color as her eyes.

"He's not wrong," Brooks murmurs, opening an umbrella I didn't even realize he was holding. "But as usual, I forget myself when I'm with you." He settles it over us, but I just pluck it from his hand and toss it to the side.

"I love the rain, Jace!" I shout as I turn toward him, sticking out my tongue. "So there!"

All of Brooks's friends—no, *my* friends now, too—start laughing.

I fight my smile as I plunk my hands on my hips and turn back to Brooks, tapping my toe. "Now what is this surprise of yours?"

He grins.

Then takes my hand and draws me into the trees. "I was going to wait until we were officially married, but"—a shrug—"I don't want to."

"Where are you going?" Rory shouts. Chrissy shushes her, but she just says, "What? They're supposed to be getting married!"

I grin and...just go with it.

Because once upon a time, I lost everything I wanted.

Because once upon a time, I never thought I'd get it back.

But I have.

And it's better than anything I've ever dreamed of.

So, I just tighten my fingers around Brooks's and let him lead me down a narrow, winding trail. Though, I am glad I opted for sneakers glittered with rhinestones instead of heels this time around.

We turn the corner and—

"Oh," I breathe.

He's led me into another clearing. Small and encircled by

huge pines, grass and wildflowers covering the ground everywhere...

Except where the trail leads.

It takes a lazy path toward a small wooden structure that had once been an old hunting cabin...

"Brooks," I whisper, my eyes burning.

That decrepit structure where I once spent the worst week of my life is gone. And in its place is something truly wonderful.

God, I love this man.

The cabin is more like a tiny house now, with glass doors and a chimney coming out of the roof, its walls covered with colorful climbing plants. But that's not the best part.

A huge copper tub sits just outside the back door.

"There's an awning that folds out so you can use it even in bad weather," he says as we draw close, pulling it out and showing me—

I gasp.

Because in the middle of the canopy, right over where I would lay in the tub, is a clear opening.

"So covered or not, you'll always be able to see the sky." He folds the awning back then shows me how the water works, along with the storage tank that will be refilled by rain before being filtered and heated, and the stack of wood that feeds the attached sauna. He's thought of every detail so the rest of the little house is just as wonderful: a small kitchenette, a linen closet with bath goodies, a cozy couch I can lay on while reading books I borrow from the shelf in the corner, and—

Freezing, I notice one more thoughtful detail.

The little square of glass positioned precisely over the couch.

So I can see the sky here too.

My eyes fill with tears.

"You like it?" he asks, swiping away one that's escaped.

I nod, press my lips to his. "It's wonderful. Thank you so much."

"Good." He reaches into his pocket then passes me an envelope.

"This isn't more blackmail material, is it?" I manage to joke, though the question is watery.

The corners of his mouth tip up. "No." He nudges a corner. "Just open it."

I do, and then—

"Dammit, Brooks," I mutter, blinking like a madwoman so I don't end up collapsing in his arms and sobbing my eyes out. Because it's the deed to this cabin...and the acreage around it.

"So you'll always have a safe space that's just yours." His mouth curves up further. "All I ask is that you let me sit in that tub with you every once in a while."

"Hmm." I tap my bottom lip, grinning. "I'll consider it."

"Consider?" he growls, snagging me around the waist and nipping at my lips. "You'll *consider* it?"

"Yup."

Another nip...followed by a deep, wet kiss that leaves me breathless.

"Still considering?" he asks.

"Absolutely."

He tugs at a lock of my hair. "Rude."

"But only because I have a very important question."

"Yeah? What's that?"

I waggle my brows. "Will you be naked when you're in the tub with me?"

"Should we find out?" he asks, slanting his lips over mine—

"Yo!" Rory shouts from outside. "We're supposed to be having a wedding!"

Giggling, I pull back and glance out the glass doors. Our

friends are all standing in the yard, blatantly spying on us. The rain has stopped, blue skies already breaking through the clouds.

"I guess we should go do that thing," I say lightly.

Brooks grins, takes my hand, and we walk toward the door. "That *thing* being marriage?"

"Exactly." I pull it open, step outside.

Which means I receive the greatest gift of all—

We get to start our happily-ever-after with laughter...

And the first rays of sunshine after a surprise summer storm.

THORN

The festivities are just getting underway inside but the woman I want is disappearing outside.

Into the darkness of Brooks's family estate.

Where it may not be safe.

Yes, he has security.

Yes, we've put measures in place to protect everyone in our circle.

Are these measures legal or moral? Not particularly.

But we've made it clear to the Lyons—fuck with one of us, and you'll live to regret it.

Still, River should be careful, shouldn't put herself at risk any more than necessary.

She's been through too much already.

Those are the thoughts running through my head as I trail her through the halls and out a set of French doors. They lead to a covered balcony that overlooks the gardens. Yup. The gardens. Brooks's ridiculous family home has gardens and a pool, an observatory and an orchard, stables and a fucking hedge maze.

River doesn't seek any of those out.

Instead, she just moves to the railing and stares out into the darkness.

For a long moment, nothing happens.

Then it's as though the armor she's been holding tightly around herself gives way. She shudders and collapses, hands clenching the railing but her body seeming to fold in on itself.

"River," I say, hurrying over to her.

But I know I've made a mistake the moment I've said her name.

Her head whips around and she straightens in an instant, her armor snapping back into place.

Damn.

"What are you doing out here?" I snap.

Her lips press flat. "Getting some air." She turns away from me, deliberately giving me her back. Fucking ignoring me.

Again.

"It's not safe," I say—another wrong thing.

Because she knows how dangerous the world can be.

Intimately.

"I'm as safe here as I am anywhere," she grits out.

That's true, and it means that I'm left wondering what to say.

Fuck, I'm always left wondering what to say when I'm with this woman.

"It's cold."

"I have a jacket."

I snort. "That can hardly be considered a jacket."

She scowls. "Seriously?"

"It's thin and doesn't even fully cover your arms."

"It's the middle of summer. It was almost ninety degrees today."

"It also rained."

A roll of her eyes before she looks back into the darkness. "Thanks for breaking down the weather for me."

Tense silence falls between us, and again I'm struck by how much I want this woman...and how little I truly know about her. Sighing, I lean back against the railing, ask softly, "Are we going to talk about it?"

Her shoulders go stiff. "There's nothing to talk about."

"You sure about that?"

She glares at me. "Yes."

"Then you won't care if I do this."

"Do wh-what?" she asks, brows flying up.

Too late.

I'm already moving, wrapping my arm around her waist, hauling her against me—

And kissing her exactly like I had that night weeks ago.

Only this time...

I don't stop.

Thank you for reading! I hope you loved Brooks and Briar's love story as much as I enjoyed writing it! The next book in the Oak Ridge series is BALLROOMS AND BLACK-MAIL **Kissing her was a mistake...only because I stopped.**

CLICK HERE TO READ BALLROOMS AND BLACKMAIL NOW>

AND IN THE MEANTIME, do you want more than a taste of those yummy Eagles hockey players? **He's the captain, I'm the owner's daughter. What could go wrong? Read** BROKEN LACES now.

AND DO you want a sneak peek into my BRAND NEW hockey series?

If you love adorable golden retriever hockey players who fall hard and fast for the women they love, pick up book one in the Grizzlies Hockey series, MARRIED TO NUMBER TWENTY-TWO NOW>. **I signed the contract. I just didn't expect her to show up ten years later, ready to cash it in.**

CLICK HERE TO READ MARRIED TO NUMBER TWENTY-TWO NOW>

READ on for a sneak peek below!

Aiden

I wake up to a heavy knock on my condo's front door and glare blearily at my phone in the charger.

"Two in the fucking morning," I mutter, grabbing a pillow and clamping it over my ears. "It's two o'clock in the morning on my fucking birthday, and I have to deal with this shit."

This shit being my neighbors.

It's not the first time they've pounded drunk on my door, desperate for their roommate to let them in to what they think is their apartment.

This was sort of funny the first time.

I remember those days, drinking too much, being dumb.

But after the second and the third—where I gained status into the inner circle and a code to the keypad to their apartment door—it was no longer cute.

Now, six months later and countless times of bailing them out, I'm *so* not in the mood.

Especially when it's my fucking birthday.

The knocking cuts off and I think—*pray*—that they've gotten the hint.

But it's approximately two seconds later when it starts up again.

I glance at my phone again, see that really five minutes have passed, making it two-seventeen and officially my birthday.

Some present.

I could try to ignore it—but that just means extending the torture. Sighing, I toss back the blankets and stomp to my apartment door, whipping it open to reveal a slender brunette on my doorstep.

"Ho, mama," she says, gaze taking a slow perusal down my body.

"Who the fuck are you?"

"It's me. Luna."

I stare at her, uncomprehendingly.

"From Rockfield?" she adds.

Recognition begins to dawn. "Luna Maybelle?"

"Yup! That's me." She nods, grinning, and I see it then, the glimpse of my best friend from the childhood rink I grew up playing at come out in her smile. Mischief and life. Joy and hard work.

Summers spent spending every spare moment together—her figure skating, me playing hockey.

But she's not little Luna anymore.

Christ, she's anything but—tall, beautiful, curves for days—and she's staring at me.

Because I'm staring at her.

Fucking hell.

I spur myself into motion.

"Luna! Oh my God!" I pull her into a hug. "What the hell are you doing here?"

"It's your birthday!" She holds up a piece of paper that looks faintly familiar. "And, well, it's mine too, remember?"

That's right.

We have the same birthday.

"We're both twenty-five, single, and—"

My eyes narrow in on the paper. It's crumpled and stained, as though it's years old.

A purple and pink swirl decorates the edges and suddenly I remember her painstakingly drawing it as we sat side-by-side at one of the high top tables of the ice rink, waiting for the Zamboni to finish cutting the ice.

Her brow had been furrowed. Her movements carefully controlled.

And I had been obsessing over how pink her lips were and what her butt looked like in her skating dress, so much so that I barely remember what we'd been drawing.

No, I think hard, grabbing on to those memories, not what we'd been *drawing*.

The contract we'd put together.

The contract my hormonal twelve-year-old self had signed.

With a sparkly pink colored pencil.

A giant boulder settles in my stomach, but before I can snap myself out of the horror of those memories, she shoves the paper in my hands then throws her arms around my neck.

"We're getting married!"

CLICK HERE TO READ MARRIED TO NUMBER TWENTY-TWO NOW>

OAK RIDGE

Hate missing Elise's new releases? Love contests, exclusive excerpts and giveaways?
Then signup for Elise's newsletter here!

***

And join Elise's fan group, the Fabinators (https://www.facebook.com/groups/fabinators) for insider information, sneak peaks at new releases, and fun freebies! Hope to see you there!

***

If you enjoy my series, considering supporting me on PATREON! Get access to early releases, bonus content, character art, audiobooks, special edition covers, swag, and much more!

CLICK HERE TO SUPPORT ME>

***

I so appreciate your help in spreading the word about my books, including sharing with friends! Please leave a review on your favorite book site!

ALSO BY ELISE FABER

Bottles & Blades

Beauty & the Boardroom

The Bachelor & the Break-in

Ballrooms and Blackmail

Gold Hockey (all stand alone)

Blocked

Backhand

Boarding

Benched

Breakaway

Breakout

Checked

Coasting

Centered

Charging

Caged

Crashed

A Gold Christmas

Cycled

Caught

Cap

Covered

Crushed

Changed

Scored

Breakers Hockey (all stand alone)

Broken

Boldly

Breathless

Ballsy

Bewitched

Blowout

Breathe

A Breakers Christmas

Blazed

Bound

Rush Hockey (read in order)

Trilogy #1

Big Puck Energy

Filthy Puckboy

So Pucking Over It

Rush Hockey Trilogy #2

Love, Pucks, and Other Stories

All's Fair in Pucks and War

No Pucks Lost Between Us

Rush Hockey Novellas

Puck and Make Up

Billionaire's Club (all stand alone)

Bad Night Stand

Bad Breakup

Bad Husband

Bad Hookup

Bad Divorce

Bad Fiancé

Bad Boyfriend

Bad Blind Date

Bad Wedding

Bad Engagement

Bad Bridesmaid

Bad Swipe

Bad Girlfriend

Bad Best Friend

Bad Rebound

Bad Romance

Bad Business

Bad Billionaire's Quickies

Love, Action, Camera (all stand alone)

Dotted Line

Action Shot

Close-Up

End Scene

Meet Cute

Love After Midnight **(all stand alone)**

Rum And Notes

Virgin Daiquiri

On The Rocks

Sex On The Seats

Life Sucks Series

Train Wreck

Hot Mess

Dumpster Fire

Clusterf*@k

FUBAR

Perfect Storm

Free Fall

Lost Cause

Roosevelt Ranch Series (all stand alone, series complete)

Disaster at Roosevelt Ranch

Heartbreak at Roosevelt Ranch

Collision at Roosevelt Ranch

Regret at Roosevelt Ranch

Desire at Roosevelt Ranch

Phoenix Series (read in order)

Phoenix Rising

Dark Phoenix

Phoenix Freed

Phoenix: LexTal Chronicles (rereleasing soon, stand alone, Phoenix world)

From Ashes

In Flames

To Smoke

KTS Series (all stand alone, series complete)

Riding The Edge

Crossing The Line

Leveling The Field

Scorching The Earth

ABOUT THE AUTHOR

USA Today bestselling author, Elise Faber, loves chocolate, Star Wars, Harry Potter, and hockey (the order depending on the day and how well her team -- the Sharks! -- are playing). She and her husband also play as much hockey as they can squeeze into their schedules, so much so that their typical date night is spent on the ice. Elise is the mom to two exuberant boys and lives in Northern California. Connect with her in her Facebook group, the Fabinators or find more information about her books at www.elisefaber.com.

f facebook.com/elisefaberauthor

a amazon.com/author/elisefaber

BB bookbub.com/profile/elise-faber

O instagram.com/elisefaber

d tiktok.com/@elisefaberauthor

g goodreads.com/elisefaber